The EXILES

‹‹‹‹‹‹‹‹‹‹‹‹‹‹‹‹‹‹‹‹‹‹‹‹‹‹‹‹

The EXILES

›››››››››››››››››››››››››

HILARY McKAY

MARGARET K. MCELDERRY BOOKS
New York

Maxwell Macmillan Canada
Toronto

Maxwell Macmillan International
New York   Oxford   Singapore   Sydney

First United States edition 1992
Copyright © 1991 by Hilary McKay
First published in Great Britain 1991 by Victor Gollancz Ltd.

Margaret K. McElderry Books
Macmillan Publishing Company
866 Third Avenue, New York, NY 10022

Maxwell Macmillan Canada, Inc.
1200 Eglinton Avenue East, Suite 200
Don Mills, Ontario M3C 3N1

Macmillan Publishing Company is part of the
Maxwell Communication Group of Companies.

Printed in the United States of America
10 9 8 7 6 5 4 3 2

Library of Congress Cataloging-in-Publication Data
McKay, Hilary.
The exiles / Hilary McKay. — 1st United States ed.
    p.   cm. "First published in Great Britain 1991
by Victor Gollancz Ltd."—T.p. verso.
Summary: The four Conroy sisters spend a wild summer at the
seaside with Big Grandma, who tries to break them of their reading
habit by substituting fresh air and hard work for books and gets
unexpected results.
ISBN 1-4169-6728-1 ISBN-13: 978-1-4169-6728-6
[1. Sisters—Fiction. 2. Grandmothers—Fiction. 3. Humorous
stories.] I. Title. PZ7.M19126Ex 1992 [Fic]—dc20 91-38220

The *EXILES*

◄◄◄◄◄◄◄◄◄◄◄◄◄◄◄◄◄◄◄◄◄◄◄◄◄

Chapter 1

‹‹‹‹‹‹‹‹‹‹‹‹‹‹‹‹‹‹‹‹‹‹‹‹‹‹

I T W A S the last weekend before the summer holidays. Naomi Conroy crouched uncomfortably at the end of the garden reading a book. As usual, she had spent her Saturday morning at the town library, searching the too familiar shelves for something new. On her left was the stack of books she had read, and on her right was the pile she hadn't opened yet. She kept her elbow leaning on that pile to guard them from her permanently book-hungry sisters. Even now, she could feel herself being watched, and without looking up knew that Ruth was hovering close by, waiting for her to finish, when by family law the book would become common property, free for anyone to read.

Ruth watched the flickering of her sister's eyes as they moved across the page. She watched Naomi's grubby fingers curl and turn the pages over. She measured the thickness of book left to read, compared it to that read already, estimated the time it would take in minutes, and sighed. Ruth was banned from the library because of the amount she owed to the library in fines.

"But I'm one of your best customers," Ruth had raged. "Worst customers," corrected the librarian. And so Ruth (who had no money) was reduced to surviving on the books her sisters chose and grudgingly handed over.

Naomi finished the chapter and closed the book. For a few seconds she could not see, and then her eyes refocused on the small, sunshiny garden. It was overcrowded, she thought. Too many plants, too many scattered belongings, too many book-starved sisters waiting to pounce.

Naomi was eleven years old, and Ruth was thirteen. They were the Big Ones. Phoebe and Rachel, aged six and eight, were the Little Ones. Although Ruth and Naomi had been known as the Big Ones since Rachel's arrival into the family, they still resented it. It gave them an uncomfortable feeling of being shoved from behind, and neither of them took kindly to being shoved.

"One more week," Ruth remarked, "and then we'll be finished with school. That'll be one less torture, anyway."

"I'd rather be at school than stuck here all summer," Naomi answered. "I'd rather do anything. Even prison would be better." She rolled over onto her back, pillowing her head on the pile of books. "Solitary confinement, everyone locked out except me, that's what I'd like."

"Anything for a change," agreed Ruth while gently easing a book away from Naomi's heap. "We ought to run away."

"I know."

"Like Robert did," said Ruth, referring to an uncle

who had made family history by disappearing in his youth and never coming back.

"Yes," agreed Naomi, "but the trouble with running away is where to run to. If we went anywhere where we know someone we'd be sent back, and if we went anywhere where we don't, then we'd be lost. It's knowing where to start."

"We'd start here," said Ruth.

"Well, then, it's knowing where to end."

"Yes."

The garden was quiet as they pondered, not for the first time, the problems of running away.

At the other end of what their father, Mr. Conroy, liked to call The Lawn, Rachel and Phoebe were racing stolen maggots around the lid of a can. The maggots belonged to Mr. Conroy and were bought for his fishing on Sundays. As well as the usual revolting white ones there were others, dyed, for some unfathomable reason, pink and green. Rachel always took a pink one, and Phoebe a green. They scooped them out of the can with the silver spoon that belonged in the tea caddy, appropriated for the purpose by Rachel. Maggot-racing already showed signs of becoming the summer's main occupation. The rules were very strict. You could prod your maggot in the right direction, but not push him forward. If they stopped you must allow them to start again of their own accord. Rachel always prodded hers with a blade of grass, but Phoebe usually favored a matchstick. Maggots responded better to matchstick-prodding, but it tended to wear them out faster. Phoebe's green maggot was beginning to look very limp.

"He's nearly dead," said Rachel.

"He's just too hot," replied Phoebe. "Anyway, I'm fed up with this. I'm going to bury him now." The career of a racing maggot inevitably ended in burial. It hid the evidence.

"Did you put the lid back on the can?" called Ruth from across the garden, remembering a time when this precaution had been forgotten, and the maggots had climbed the impossibly smooth sides of the can, and escaped all over the toolshed.

"Did we?" asked Phoebe.

"Hope not," said Naomi as Rachel hurried away to check, "we could do with a bit of excitement."

Phoebe finished patting the earth smooth over the maggot's grave and remarked, "I wish something would happen."

"Well, it won't," said Ruth.

Mr. and Mrs. Conroy didn't own a car, wouldn't buy a television, disliked the thought of allowing pets into an already chaotic household, and could never quite afford to go on holidays. Naturally this made things somewhat difficult for their daughters, who, partly from personal inclination and partly in self-defense, maintained a carefully fostered defiance toward the world in general and school in particular.

THE WEEKEND drifted on, exhausting itself and its participants with nonevents. Sunday afternoon ended in Sunday dinner, varied and bountiful, and prepared, as always, by Mrs. Conroy alone with no help from her daughters. The evening ran its usual course. Mrs. Conroy dragged her husband from under his newspaper to spray the roses, her daughters from behind their library books to finish their homework, school clothes from where they'd been flung on Friday to be exclaimed over in horror, and afterward, having found occupations for everybody but herself, sat down and watched them work.

"I don't think this day will ever end." She sighed.

Rachel and Phoebe were bathed, clean-pajamaed, and got rid of.

Naomi toiled through the dregs of her homework and was dismissed.

Ruth escaped.

Mr. and Mrs. Conroy, after cups of weak tea and milk-chocolate biscuits, locked the doors and withdrew.

RACHEL AND PHOEBE slept in bunk beds packed with teddy bears, coloring books, and stray lumps of Lego. Phoebe in the bottom bunk dreamed of crocodiles, the ones that lived in the front room behind the settee. There was nothing to be afraid of as long as you poked potato chips into their mouths, and there were plenty of potato chips left over from dinner. Happily in her sleep Phoebe fed the dream crocodiles. Beneath the bedclothes her fingers moved, picking up chips. Phoebe was safe in the dark; it never frightened her. Sometimes she woke herself up, singing loudly.

Rachel, in the top bunk because she was the elder of the two, slept with her back jammed against the wall as far from the edge as possible. It was very uncomfortable. She had fallen asleep with her face resting on her hard brown braid, and it was printing a pattern of twists across her cheek. She did not dream, but all through her sleep felt a nervous distrust of the edge of the bed.

The dark was thickest and blackest in Ruth and Naomi's room, where huge, old, blue velvet curtains hung, smothering the windows. The curtains had faded around the hems to a browny gray color, and they held in Ruth and Naomi and the dark like jailers.

Ruth lay awake, staring at nothing and thinking. One day, she would spend summer in the countryside, somewhere hilly, not like the Lincolnshire flatness she was accustomed to. She would have two houses—one for herself, and one for her family to come and visit her in— and she would be a famous . . . a famous . . . a famous what? Well, famous anyway, and very rich of course . . .

"Are you awake?" hissed Naomi through the dark.

"I'm thinking."

"What about?"

"When I'm rich."

"Huh!"

Silence for a while.

"Is that all you're thinking about?" asked Naomi eventually.

"One more week of school."

"Yucky-pucky," said Naomi, and fell asleep.

Chapter 2

‹‹‹‹‹‹‹‹‹‹‹‹‹‹‹‹‹‹‹‹‹‹‹‹‹‹‹‹

RETURNING FROM WORK for his lunch on Monday, Mr. Conroy found Mrs. Conroy anxiously peering down the street, clutching the first ever lawyer's letter delivered to disturb the household. Evidently she was talking to herself, for her lips were moving.

"Wonder and worry," he heard as he came up to her, "I've done nothing but wonder and worry all morning. Thank goodness you're home at last," she said, distractedly kissing the air beside his ear and thrusting a long white envelope into his hands. "I'm sure there's nothing you've done and I know the girls can be naughty, but they're not that bad that anyone should want to . . . Well, for Heaven's sake, John, patting my back won't help anything! Open it up and tell me the worst!"

Mr. Conroy ceased attempting to calm his wife and studied the address on the corner of the envelope.

"Never heard of them," he remarked and began carefully unsealing the flap so as not to tear it.

"Do hurry, John!"

"It looks like," said Mr. Conroy after hastily scanning the first page, "my poor old uncle's dead. ...."

"Well, it's the first I've heard of you having a poor old uncle," replied his wife, sighing with relief and bending to read the page he held out to her.

Mr. Conroy, after quickly working it out on his fingers, explained that he hadn't actually an uncle, but he had a great-aunt (who had been gone for years), and she had married for a second time late in life. Which would mean, concluded Mr. Conroy, that he had a great-step-uncle whom he'd never met.

"And never will now," added Mrs. Conroy as she finished reading.

"They'll be wanting us to help with the funeral expenses," said Mr. Conroy in the melancholy tone of one who has lost an unknown relative and gained a large bill.

"Really, John," exclaimed Mrs. Conroy crossly, "why must you always think the worst! Read the letter and stop talking rubbish!"

Still standing on the doorstep, feeling rather bemused and getting very hungry, Mr. Conroy took the letter back and turned to the second page, reading it partly to himself, and partly out loud to his wife.

"Bequests include fifty thousand pounds and all property to his home help," remarked Mr. Conroy, showing no emotion at this revelation. "Very nice for her.

"Fifty thousand pounds to Cats' Protection League.

"Fifty thousand pounds toward paying off the national debt," continued Mr. Conroy. "He must have been quite a character.

"Ten thousand pounds to each surviving nephew or niece. That would have pleased my mother.

"Five thousand pounds to each surviving great-nephew or niece!"

"That's you!" said Mrs. Conroy.

"Well, fancy him thinking of me!" Mr. Conroy looked up, beaming. "And you've been getting yourself so upset! It's about the best thing that ever happened to me! After marrying you," he added gallantly, seeing Mrs. Conroy's face.

"And the girls," prompted Mrs. Conroy. "And I'm bound to be a bit upset after the morning I've had and now thinking he's gone and we shan't be able to thank him, and as for him leaving all that money to those cats and that home help . . ."

"Well, don't worry about them," said Mr. Conroy sensibly. "What about our bit? Think what the girls are going to say!"

They both thought about what the girls would say.

"I don't know if we should tell them anything about it," said Mrs. Conroy eventually. "There'll be no peace at all, once they find out. We ought to just keep quiet until we decide what to do."

Mr. Conroy quite agreed. "And then we'll surprise them," he said.

THAT EVENING a strange thing happened in the Conroy household. Instead of cold meat left over from Sunday, for supper they had steak and mushrooms.

"Why?" asked the girls. "What's today?"

Their parents were not exactly smiling, but they had a complacent look about them.

"You deserve a treat now and then," they said. It was all a bit mysterious.

* * *

DURING THE COURSE of breakfast on Tuesday morning Rachel and Phoebe remarked several times that they needed shopping bags to take to school that day.

"Why?" asked Mrs. Conroy, who could never find a bag when she wanted one. Then, noticing the grass stains on her daughters' dresses for the first time, she added, "What on earth have you been doing? You look like goodness knows what! Why didn't you put your clothes in the wash last night? Go and take them off!"

"The teachers said to bring shopping bags," Phoebe told her, patiently persisting in sticking to the main issue even while being hauled back up to her bedroom.

"Well, you can tell them"—Mrs. Conroy pulled Phoebe's dress over her head without unbuttoning it, so that Phoebe's ears nearly came off—"that I'm not supplying them with shopping bags. They've just had all that jam for the bazaar! They're always wanting something at that school. Rachel! Just look at your knees! Green! Wash them!"

"They're to put our pictures and projects in," Rachel explained, vaguely licking her knees and rubbing them with a sock as she spoke. "Everyone's got to take them, to bring their pictures and projects home." It was a triumph that Rachel had been looking forward to for weeks.

"Well, I suppose I might manage to find one for you," Mrs. Conroy said grudgingly as she finished buttoning up Phoebe and gave her a gentle smack to start her off.

"Can I have two?" asked Phoebe.

"Can I borrow your big shopping bag?" asked Rachel, regarding her knees with satisfaction. "I've got an awful lot to bring home."

"You can get off to school, the pair of you," ordered Mrs. Conroy, hurrying them back downstairs, where she dug out a couple of bags. "Look at the time! And I've got so much to do today. Give me a kiss, it's time you were gone. And make sure you bring those bags back. And don't go bringing a lot of rubbish home with you!"

"It's our pictures and projects," said Rachel, hurt dreadfully at this remark. "Nearly all my pictures have been on the wall."

"Mine's mostly rubbish," agreed Phoebe cheerfully, "but I'm bringing it home, anyway. There's too much to throw away. I've been saving it for you."

Mrs. Conroy sighed at the thought as she shepherded them out of the house. "Cross the road with the safety lady," she called.

"Don't you want to see my pictures and projects?" asked Rachel mournfully, but her mother had already closed the door.

RUTH AND NAOMI arrived back that afternoon to find their mother at the gate, impatiently waiting for Rachel and Phoebe to return.

"They're bringing their bags of junk home," Ruth reminded her. "That's what's taking them so long."

"You two go and meet them and give them a hand then," her mother replied. "They should have been home half an hour ago. I think they walk more slowly every day."

"It's the weight of their brains," remarked Naomi.

They found their little sisters three quarters of the way back already, a weary looking pair, travel stained and burdened by the fruits of a year's industrious paperwork. Phoebe had a newly skinned knee that still trickled blood down onto her sock, and both of them bore traces of recently dried tears on their cheeks. Bulging shopping bags weighed them down, and they hugged uncurling rolls of pictures under their arms, while between them they carried a huge paper-and-balsa-wood model of the town center that had been constructed by the entire school in the course of several weeks' geography lessons. It looked very heavy, and had obviously been dropped many times already. A lot of the houses and the entire church tower had come loose and were lying in the river, which was a real river, lined with a plastic bag and filled with water. Even now not all the water had leaked away.

Rachel and Phoebe lowered their prize carefully to the ground and stood waiting for their sisters.

"Look what we've got," said Rachel proudly. "They gave it to us to share."

"They gave it to us *for nothing*," stressed Phoebe, "and it's probably worth pounds and pounds!"

"Well, I'm going," said Naomi after one horrified glance. "Somebody might see me with you. Unless you promise to leave it there and walk quietly away."

"I think," said Ruth from the curbstone where she was sitting to enable her to laugh in comfort, "we'll probably be arrested if we just leave it here." Rachel and Phoebe started to cry. It had been a hard journey.

"Don't you think it's lovely?" wailed Rachel.

"Pick up the other side, Naomi," ordered Ruth, "and we'll run with it as fast as we can."

"Me?" asked Naomi. "Carry that thing?"

"Yes, quick, before anyone comes."

"Damn!" said Naomi gloomily, but picking up her end nevertheless. "I wish I'd never come! Well, let's run fast and get it over with."

So they ran fast, and Rachel and Phoebe followed screeching, "You'll break it! You'll spill the water!" while they stooped to pick up stray trees and house roofs, and dropped their rolls of paper every time they bent.

"T H E Y *must* be mad at that school!" said Mrs. Conroy when she saw her daughters. "Letting you cart home a thing like that. I don't know what they're thinking of, and I'd go and tell them so if I wasn't so busy this week. And where do you think you're taking it?" she asked Rachel, who had got hold of one end of the construction and was bumping it up the stairs, leaving a trail of flaked-off paint behind her.

"Nowhere," answered Rachel, who got more like her big sisters every day.

"You'll have to put it in the garden—it can stay there until the trashmen come. I'll have to ask them to take it specially."

Rachel and Phoebe started mechanically to cry, Phoebe reflecting that it got easier to make real tears every time.

"My class painted the streets and grass," she whimpered.

"Very badly," commented Naomi dispassionately. "Why are the banks of the river purple?"

"Why can't I ever have anything?" Rachel snuffled. "Why can't I take it upstairs? Why can't I have it to play with for the summer?"

"We'll have more than enough mess in the house this summer as it is," answered Mrs. Conroy. "Take it outside for now, anyway. I don't know what's the matter with you both, wailing like babies. Perhaps you'd better go to bed!"

"Why will we have more than enough mess this summer as it is?" asked Naomi, who had been wondering what was in the air ever since the steak and mushrooms.

"What's for supper tonight?" asked Ruth. If it was another exotic meal, she decided, something must be afoot.

"Cold meat and chips," said Mrs. Conroy, squashing her hopes, "or . . ."

"What?" asked Ruth and Naomi together.

"Egg and chips," said Mrs. Conroy, "and someone come and help."

" Y o u r father and I want a few minutes in peace," said Mrs. Conroy after supper that night.

"And out of hearing," added Mr. Conroy.

Reluctantly, Ruth and Naomi took themselves off into the garden, where Rachel and Phoebe sat in the evening sunshine surrounded by schoolwork dating back to the previous September. For as long as they could manage they ignored this unenticing array of knowledge, but eventually Rachel, by continual repetition of the same question, succeeded in luring them over.

"Here's an Easter card I made for you," said Rachel by way of a bribe to Ruth.

"Thanks," said Ruth. "What's that dog doing coming out of that egg?"

"I thought you liked dogs. Look, here's my dinosaur project."

" 'A long time ago all our grandparents were monkeys,' " Ruth read aloud, " 'but before that it was all dinosaurs.' "

"That's all wrong, then," said Naomi. "Look at Big Grandma. She's a dinosaur now!"

"Don't you like Big Grandma?" asked Phoebe.

"No," said Naomi.

"You won't either when you're older," said Ruth wisely.

"I don't now," said Phoebe. "She says I'm spoiled!"

"She says we all are," Naomi agreed, "and that we read too much and answer back and never do anything to help."

"Last time she was here," added Ruth, "she said we'd soon know the difference if we lived with her and I said, 'I expect it would be lovely, Grandma,' and she said 'Don't kid yourself.' "

"She talks like that to make herself feel modern," explained Naomi. "I don't blame Uncle Robert a bit for running away. I would have. If I could have thought of anywhere to run to. What's this?"

"My Christmas-present list," Phoebe told her.

It read:

> A train set
> A black velvet cloke

A donkey
A television
A sack of Ester Eggs
A swimming pool not to depe
My own magots

The Easter eggs, swimming pool, and maggots were obviously later additions.

"Imagine anyone keeping a Christmas-present list up to date," said Ruth. "Since last December! When did you add the maggots?"

"Yesterday. I tick things off when I get them."

"Nothing's been ticked off."

"I know. Give it back. I still need it."

"What for?"

"Next year."

Mr. Conroy appeared at the back door and shouted, "Bedtime, Rachel and Phoebe, and pick all that mess up before you come in!"

"Don't you want to see my pictures and projects?" asked Rachel.

"I'm going to put that on your gravestone," remarked Naomi. "Rachel Conroy. Born first of February. Don't you want to see my pictures and projects? And then the date you die."

THE SHADOW of the garden wall was gradually covering the lawn, and Ruth and Naomi were retreating in front of it. The talcum powder smell of night-scented stocks drifted through the air. Ruth sat in a daydream, her mind running over the talk of Big Grandma and

Uncle Robert, whom Naomi did not blame for running away.

"Why don't you blame Uncle Robert?" she demanded suddenly. "I do. He should have at least written or something. He should have come back, not just left everybody wondering."

She looked across at Naomi, who sat reading, all hunched up with her sweater buttoned over her knees, her head bent, and her straight brown hair falling in screens on either side of her face.

"He was in a bad temper," said Naomi eventually.

"Fancy staying in a bad temper for thirty years! He must have hated Big Grandma!"

"I expect that's what she thinks." Ruth lost interest and changed the subject. "They haven't got the radio on indoors you know. They're just talking and talking. And I can't work out about that steak and stuff. I've thought and thought and all I can think of is that it might be another baby."

"Can't be," said Naomi immediately, "because they were very pleased with themselves last night and they wouldn't be pleased if they thought they were getting another one of us. They think we're enough."

It grew colder in the garden as the patch of shadow gradually nudged them toward the flower bed. When it finally tipped them into it, they gave up speculating and went indoors.

MR. AND MRS. CONROY sat late into the night, turning the pages of glossy-printed catalogs and talking.

"I can hardly believe it's going to happen!"

"Should have it all in place by autumn if we can get started straight away."

"It would be a terrible job trying to keep the girls out of the way. And I don't know how I'll manage cooking for a family with all this going on."

"What about that offer then? Still deciding?"

"It's not likely they've ever been by themselves before."

"Won't be much of a summer for them here, and it would be a break for you, too. And me. We'll pretend we're young again."

"It's not like they got on with her when she was here. It was a shocking week, practically open warfare by the time she left."

"She tried to reform them too quickly. Not that a bit of reforming would come amiss. But I think she'd be upset if you refused her."

"I know she would."

"And it's a smashing place. They're always wanting to be off somewhere else in the summer, too."

"I know they are."

"It's not as if they were bad kids. On the whole."

"It's not as if they were good ones either!"

"Well, we'll have to just keep thinking about it."

"I know," said Mrs. Conroy.

Chapter 3

◀◀◀◀◀◀◀◀◀◀◀◀◀◀◀◀◀◀◀◀◀◀◀

"THREE MORE DAYS," remarked Ruth at breakfast time on Wednesday morning.

"Then what?" asked Phoebe.

"Nothing, probably." Naomi's tone of extreme gloom and pessimism caused Mr. and Mrs. Conroy to glance momentarily at each other. Mr. Conroy raised his eyebrows, but his wife shook her head, still undecided. It was Rachel who finally helped her make up her mind to do it to them.

Last year at the end of school Mrs. Conroy had said to Rachel, "Don't you *ever* dare say that you'll clear up those horrible paint things again!"

Rachel's school dress had been ruined; the stains left from school powder paint never do wash out. Rachel remembered very clearly all the fuss that had been made and so when this year the teacher said, "Let me see who I can ask to tidy up the paint things for us," and she had shot up her hand and said, "Oh, please me," before any of the other children could speak, she did at least feel guilty.

But not very guilty.

Alone in the girls' toilet with a handbasin full of water and the paint things full of sin beside her, Rachel began the hour of doom.

Very carefully she washed the brushes, and then the jam jars, and the palettes that didn't have much paint on them. It was pleasant with the warm water, and the sunshine glowing through the windows and the buzzing sound from the surrounding classrooms. Happily Rachel started on the palettes that contained something worth washing. She lowered a full one into the basin and turned the water dark blue, and then tipped in yellow to make it green. It took a lot of yellow to make it even faintly greenish. Red slipped in and the water went very dark, so she added a lot of other colors, trying to make black. After that she emptied the basin and held the palettes under the tap, watching the colors stream out and swim together and run down the plug hole. She nearly put her finger up the end of the tap to make it spray, but then thought better of it and didn't. Too soon everything was shining clean and she had nothing left except a yogurt carton half full of bright red that she had been saving till last. Carefully she poured it into a sink full of clean water, glowing with pleasure at the beautiful pink that resulted. Then she let the water out and dried her hands.

"Goodness, Rachel!" exclaimed the teacher, coming in to hurry her up. "Couldn't you have been a bit more careful?"

Rachel looked at her in amazement.

"Just look at your dress!" said the teacher.

Rachel looked down and could not believe what she

was seeing. She was covered in paint again, just like last year. Just like last year, only worse. There was even paint on her socks, and all over the splashes and drips of color on her dress she saw a complete set of red fingermarks wiped right down her front. It was like being haunted.

"Well, it's a good thing it's going-home time," said the teacher. "Why didn't you put an overall on?"

Rachel did not answer. She was suffering from shock. Going home Phoebe said, "You've got paint on your dress."

Phoebe didn't often notice things about other people.

"Leave me alone," said Rachel.

"What d'you think Mum'll say?" asked Phoebe conversationally.

"Leave me alone!"

"She didn't say anything about the grass marks. Hardly anything. Everybody else's mum did. Jacqueline Draper's mum hit her!"

Rachel continued to plod along the street in silence.

"Hit her," repeated Phoebe, glancing sideways at Rachel. "On her head!" she added, hoping to extract a response. "With a frying pan! Eleven times!" (Phoebe saw nothing wrong in occasionally stretching the truth.)

"I bet Mum hits you this time!" she said cheerfully as they reached home.

Rachel watched sourly as Phoebe disappeared through the front door, and then she trudged around to the back of the house alone. Mrs. Conroy was in the kitchen talking to a strange man who appeared to be measuring the walls. Rachel stood in the doorway, scrabbling through her mind for an opening remark, but as it turned out she did not need to say anything at all. Mrs. Conroy, catching sight of her daughter's miserable face, and the red streaks, rushed across to her.

"You've hurt yourself," she cried in concern.

"S'paint," said Rachel.

"Ooh dearie me," remarked the man, and started writing busily on a little pad so that he wouldn't have to have anything to do with it.

"Well," said Mrs. Conroy straightening up. "That's the second dress this week! Didn't I tell you! Look at the state . . . ! This really *is* the last straw!"

True to Phoebe's prediction, Mrs. Conroy smacked Rachel, and then got crosser still because she and Mr. Conroy had agreed never to smack Rachel and Phoebe— this was because they had done so with Ruth and Naomi on occasion and it had never achieved the slightest good. (Ruth and Naomi strongly opposed the new policy.)

Rachel howled unnecessarily loudly, considering it had only been one slap, not hard, nor on her head, nor with a frying pan.

"You can just stay like that until your father comes home and we'll see what he has to say!"

Rachel stopped howling to argue.

"I don't want to hear," interrupted Mrs. Conroy. "I'm very busy. Go outside and behave yourself."

Rachel sat on the grass and wished she was dead. She held her breath to suffocate herself to death but as soon as it began to hurt she couldn't help breathing again.

Naomi will write on my gravestone, she thought miserably. She said she would, and she took another breath to try again. Behind her Naomi said:

"What's the man doing in the kitchen?"

No peace, thought Rachel. Nobody will even leave me alone to kill myself.

"Rachel," said Ruth, "what's that man doing in the kitchen? Mum won't let us in."

"Measuring," answered Rachel, gasping for air, "leave me alone."

"Measuring what? Come on, tell us. We saw you in there."

"Measuring the walls. Leave me alone."

"If you're worried about that paint," said Naomi kindly, "you're wasting your time. That dress was thirdhand, anyway, and no one but our family would be seen dead in it. It's a good thing it's ruined. At least Phoebe will escape it."

"Is it ruined?" asked Ruth with interest.

"Bound to be," said Naomi cheerfully, "that paint never washes off."

"It does," said Rachel.

"No, I don't think it does," contradicted Ruth, "because remember that one you did last year. Mum just threw it away. It's quite a good way of getting rid of them."

"I didn't want it, anyway," added Phoebe, doing her bit to cheer her sister up. "It looked awful on."

"Are you sure he's measuring the walls?" asked Ruth, returning to her original question.

"No. I didn't really look."

"It's no good talking to her when she's got that dress on," said Naomi. "Go and take it off, Rachel."

"I've got to keep it on until Dad comes home."

"Why?" asked Naomi. "He won't want to see it. Go and take it off."

"Can I say you made me?" asked Rachel cautiously.

"Anything," said Naomi. "Get it off and then go and listen outside the kitchen door."

"Well? Did you hear anything?" Ruth asked when Rachel returned a few minutes later.

"No. Nothing that made sense. I can't remember it, anyway."

"Why on earth have you got your pajamas on? It's not even five o'clock. Are you ill?"

"I thought I'd probably be sent to bed," Rachel replied, "so I thought I might as well get ready."

Her sisters looked at her in despair. They believed in behaving as though they were innocent at least until they were proven guilty, and quite often even after that.

"It was a very weak-spirited thing to do," pronounced Naomi pompously, "especially when I said you could say that I made you."

"Go and get changed again," ordered Ruth. "You've got to learn to stick up for yourself whatever you've done!"

"Can I say you made me?" asked Rachel, slowly getting to her feet again.

"If you must." Ruth sighed as she watched her sister trudge once more to the house.

"No moral strength," remarked Naomi.

"I know," said Ruth, "but she's got to be trained."

"She's lucky to have us, really," said Naomi.

"THERE SHE WAS, covered in paint," related Mrs. Conroy late that night, when explaining her heartless behavior to her husband, "and Ruth and Naomi just encouraging her to misbehave, and I suddenly thought it wouldn't hurt them at all."

"Do them the world of good," agreed Mr. Conroy.

"And as for what happened when we told them!"

For suppertime, when the news of the sudden wealth of the Conroy family had been broken, had been rather tense.

"I AM GOING to make a family announcement," Mr. Conroy had begun. Ruth and Naomi glanced at each other.

"What?" asked Rachel, forgetting she was in disgrace and stabbing a whole sausage onto her fork.

"Use your *knife!*" scolded Mrs. Conroy as Rachel bit the sausage in half, "and I thought I told you not to get changed!"

"Ruth and Naomi made me!"

"What announcement?" asked Naomi.

"Go on, John, tell them," Mrs. Conroy said.

Mr. Conroy told them.

For a few moments his daughters sat around the table in complete silence, too surprised to move, too surprised to think, staring at their parents in amazement. Phoebe's mashed potato fell off her fork onto the tablecloth and Rachel picked it up and ate it without even knowing what she was doing.

"That's taken the wind from your sails," said Mr. Conroy. "I must say it rather did mine when I first heard it."

"Why'd he leave it to us?" asked Rachel. "He doesn't even know us."

27

"Because we're his family," explained Mrs. Conroy, "or your father is, but it's the same thing. Not that it all went to family, not by any means!"

"Five thousand pounds!" repeated Rachel. "Five thousand pounds! It's the first time I've ever been rich!"

Ruth started to think quickly. Five thousand pounds between six. That was, six eights are forty-eight, so six eight hundreds are forty-eight hundred, and that was still less than five thousand pounds. More than eight hundred pounds each! She would buy a horse and still have plenty left to get it food and a stable. Where did one buy a horse from? She would have to get someone to help. Lots of people would probably be glad to.

"Eight hundred and thirty pounds each!" said Naomi, who had also been calculating. "When do we get it?"

Rachel was thinking, I need some money. She wasn't sure exactly what for, but she knew she never had anything like enough. She started trying to remember all the things she had always wanted.

Phoebe had mentally gone through her Christmas-present list and decided she could buy everything on it. She could hardly wait to tick them off.

Mrs. Conroy said, "We've decided to have the kitchen enlarged this summer. It will mean knocking down the pantry wall of course, and we're having the outside of the house painted, and new bathroom fixtures put in. It's going to mean having workmen in the house for a few weeks, but still, summer is the best time for getting work like that done."

"That'll be nice," said Ruth politely, but not really listening, "I'm buying a horse with mine."

"You're not going to have much left," remarked Naomi to her mother, "or are you and Dad clubbing together to get all that done?"

"Can I have mine now?" asked Rachel.

"Your what?"

"My eight hundred and thirty pounds," repeated Rachel patiently. "I need it now."

Mr. Conroy laughed and pulled her braid. "Poor old Rachel," he said, "did you think you were suddenly rich?"

Ruth and Naomi immediately stopped their joyful gloating and looked at their parents. Ruth remembered that she had felt like this once before, the time she had fallen straight over her bike's handlebars. The moment before she hit the ground.

Naomi stared across at her smiling father and suspicion hardened into certainty. She tried to speak, but found she couldn't because her mouth was already hanging open.

"What's up, Naomi?" asked her father, still cheerful.

"What! D'you mean you're not sharing it?" demanded Naomi. "D'you mean you're keeping it all for yourselves?"

Tears filled Ruth's eyes as she watched the chestnut pony with black mane and tail gallop away to nowhere.

"I bet they're wasting it all on the blasted house!" she said sadly, guessing nothing but the miserable truth.

"Whatever are you thinking of?" asked Mrs. Conroy crossly. "Speaking like that! We thought you'd be pleased. Of course we're sharing it—you all live here, don't you? You'll enjoy it as much as we will!"

"Oh, my money," whispered Rachel as tears began to pour down her cheeks.

"It's ours as much as yours," stormed Naomi, "you said he left it to the family. It's a beastly, mean, rotten, thieving, horrible thing to do, and I hope he comes back and haunts you!"

"Naomi!"

"Stolen already!" sobbed Rachel.

"Typical, typical, typical," lamented Ruth.

Phoebe, who still didn't understand, asked, "Why can't Rachel have her money? Because she got all covered in paint?" She looked at Rachel's betrayed face and didn't think it was fair.

"You can have some of mine, Rachel," she offered. How much her Christmas list was going to come to she had no idea, but if there wasn't enough she could always skip the cloak. It wasn't really the weather for velvet cloaks, anyway. "Tell me what you want and I'll buy it, Rachel," she said magnanimously.

"I think you ought to explain to Phoebe," said Naomi coldly. "She still thinks you're going to be honest!"

"Stop being so ridiculous all of you!" exclaimed Mrs. Conroy, suddenly losing her temper. "This house is going to be redecorated this summer, and while it's being done you four will be going to stay with Grandma"— Mr. Conroy looked very pleased—"and . . ."

"What Grandma? Big Grandma, d'you mean?" asked Ruth, horrified.

"You'll have a splendid time," said Mr. Conroy.

"Is it a joke?" asked Naomi, "because it's not very funny if it is."

"Big Grandma doesn't like us," remarked Rachel dismally.

"Of course she does, when you behave yourselves, anyway," Mr. Conroy replied, speaking horribly cheerfully to cover up how guilty he was feeling.

"Is it true?" asked Naomi. "Just tell me whether it's true or not."

"I shall take you up there by train on Saturday," said Mrs. Conroy, throwing all her former caution to the winds. "You've been wanting to go away this summer, and now you are going. And it's no use you arguing," she added, "because it's all arranged. So you might as well make the best of it."

"You'll have a wonderful time; summer by the sea in Cumbria," Mr. Conroy said encouragingly.

"Big Grandma," said Ruth, "thinks we're awful. You should have heard what she said to me last time she was here."

"Are we going to stay with Big Grandma?" asked Phoebe. "Why? She says I'm spoiled! I'm not going!"

"You all are," Mr. Conroy said, "and we expect you Big Ones to help take care of the Little Ones."

"Can I take my money?" Phoebe asked.

Rachel was crying again.

Ruth and Naomi escaped from the table and went up to their bedroom and shut the door. As soon as they were able, Rachel and Phoebe followed after them. They had great faith in their big sisters, who so far had never let them down. Very unhappy, but not quite despairing, they climbed the stairs.

Mr. Conroy said to Mrs. Conroy, "I never thought they'd expect a share, did you?"

"They'll soon forget it," Mrs. Conroy comforted him. "They've plenty to take their minds off it. Don't you worry."

Upstairs, nobody said anything.

"RUTH AND NAOMI will think of something."

Rachel and Phoebe consoled themselves constantly with this thought, for in the past their sisters had rescued them from so many impossible situations. Not that the solutions provided by Ruth and Naomi necessarily improved matters, far from it in most cases. Still, they generally managed to alter and enliven the course of events.

"HAVEN'T YOU THOUGHT of anything yet?" demanded Rachel in a hoarse whisper as the taxi carried them to the station on Saturday.

"No," replied Ruth crossly. "All we can do is pretend we don't care."

"How?" asked Rachel.

"WE'VE GOT TO PRETEND we don't care," Rachel told Phoebe on the train. "They're sending us away to Big Grandma, who hates us, for six whole weeks so that they can spend our money in peace, and we've got to pretend we don't care. How?"

Phoebe, who had never been on a train before, scarcely listened. Six weeks must be a long time, she supposed, since school had closed down as if forever. Going to Big Grandma's was very bad news, but it hadn't quite happened yet, and she still had hopes that it never would. What else was Rachel grumbling about? Money. Her Christmas-present list money that they still hadn't given her.

"I want a serious word with you girls," announced Mrs. Conroy.

Perhaps she's going to give it to me now, thought Phoebe.

"I do not want to hear," said Mrs. Conroy ominously, "of any sort of trouble from you four. The fuss you've all been making about this holiday is nothing short of ridiculous. You'll find you will have a wonderful time. . . ."

"I've brought this to put it in," interrupted Phoebe, producing her now-empty pictures-and-projects shopping bag.

"Don't be silly, Phoebe. I hope to goodness you'll come back with a bit more sense. I'm sure your grandma won't put up with half the nonsense your father and I let you get away with."

"I expect that's why Uncle Robert ran away," put in Ruth gloomily.

"And you are *not*," continued Mrs. Conroy, "to mention Robert at all! Do you understand? I won't have your grandma upset by you."

"What about Big Grandma upsetting us?" asked Naomi.

"And another thing," said Mrs. Conroy, "you can make up your minds to stop calling her by that silly name."

"We've all got silly names," Ruth pointed out.

"You were never such worries when you were babies," said Mrs. Conroy regretfully.

"We never had so many things to worry us then," Naomi said. "Does she know we're coming?"

Sometimes Mrs. Conroy could not believe the idiocy of her own daughters.

Chapter 4

‹‹‹‹‹‹‹‹‹‹‹‹‹‹‹‹‹‹‹‹‹‹‹‹‹‹‹

IT WAS DIFFICULT to remember who had first chris-
tened Big Grandma. None of the children had ever
thought of her as anything else; yet it could not have
been their parents because they did not like the name at
all. Anyway, they called her that now, without thinking
what it meant, or even meaning to be rude.

There were plenty of reasons why she should be called
Big Grandma. For a start she was very tall and muscly,
and she ate a lot. Also, she wore men's pajamas and
drank whiskey at bedtime. In a lot of ways she was huge.
Her house was very big, too; even the toilet was higher
than ordinary people's toilets. It had a wooden seat
which always felt warm, and by Monday morning
Naomi had decided that the only thing she really liked
about Big Grandma's house was the toilet seat.

On Monday morning, Mrs. Conroy, who had traveled
up with the children primarily to make sure they got
there, and didn't escape on the way (as she had heard
them planning to do), caught an early train back home
to Lincolnshire. Big Grandma drove her to the station

in her awful car and refused to let the girls come, too. Mrs. Conroy said she didn't want any scenes on the platform, and Big Grandma said they would be more trouble than they were worth. Just before she drove away she shouted:

"Hurry up and have breakfast ready for when I come back! You'll find everything you need! Two eggs for me!"

Then she tooted her beastly horn and drove off with their mother. They didn't even have time to wave good-bye.

They were left alone.

"She's gone!" Phoebe said. Until that moment she had never really believed her mother would leave them there. Suddenly she started running after the car. She ran and ran, but already the car was out of sight. Giving up, she stood deserted in the middle of the empty road. Ruth and Naomi came puffing to meet her.

"Don't start crying for goodness' sake!" implored Ruth. "You'll only set Rachel off!"

"I'm not," said Phoebe indignantly. "I wanted to catch Mum. She forgot to give me my Christmas-list money."

Naomi abandoned self-control and grabbed her deluded little sister by the shoulders.

"Look at me!"

Phoebe stared disinterestedly at Naomi's flat chest.

"At my face!"

Phoebe gazed upward.

"Now listen. You are not getting *any* money! Do you understand?"

Phoebe privately decided that Naomi was mad, but nevertheless nodded appeasingly.

"Say yes," commanded Naomi.

"Yes," agreed Phoebe casually, and then as Naomi released her grip she added cheerfully, "I'll get it when we go home then."

Rachel was standing on the front steps looking very miserable. "What about breakfast?" she called as they frogmarched Phoebe up to her. "She said she wanted two eggs."

"I don't know. We didn't have any yesterday, getting up so late. How are we to know where she keeps everything?"

"Big Grandma had a big breakfast yesterday," Phoebe remarked. "She had bacon and stuff like that. I smelled it cooking."

"Well, we'd better do something," Ruth said, heading back through the house to the kitchen. "She'll be here soon, and she'll only start gloating and swaggering if we don't."

"And calling us incapable," agreed Naomi. "Come on then."

Tentatively they started opening cupboard doors and exploring the contents. They found a lot of homemade jam in one, and another full of herbs and spices.

"Look at all this curry powder," said Ruth. "Whatever does she want that amount for?"

"She probably cleans her teeth with it," Naomi replied. "Here's eggs, ordinary ones, and horrible looking ones. I suppose we ought to give her the ordinaries."

"I want Frosties," Phoebe announced.

"Look what I've found," called Rachel. "Dog food! I didn't know Big Grandma had a dog!"

"There aren't any Frosties," said Ruth. "I can't even find cornflakes. What's that you've got, Rachel?"

"Cans of dog food. D'you think she's got a dog?"

"We'd have seen it yesterday." A nasty thought struck Ruth and she hastened to share it. "Perhaps she eats it herself."

"Probably it's for when she turns into a werewolf," Naomi suggested, "and hasn't any grandchildren to chew on."

"Shut up," said Ruth. "Help me set the table so it looks like we've done something."

She fetched five plates and set them around the table. Rachel found bread in a can marked RUBBISH in which she had been searching for empty dog food cans. Naomi put five knives beside the plates and the loaf of bread in the middle of the table with the bread knife beside it.

"She'll have to have boiled eggs," said Ruth. "I don't think I can do any other sort." Then Naomi discovered an egg cup and put one of the eggs in it. She put the other in a saucepan of cold water and stood it on the stove.

"It's no good cooking it until she comes in."

They stood back to have a look at the table. It seemed a bit bare. Phoebe fetched salt and pepper and vinegar all together in a silver stand and placed it carefully in the middle next to the bread, just as they heard the front door open.

Ruth noticed the butter on the sideboard and plonked it hurriedly beside the bread. That was all they could do.

"Rachel!" bellowed Big Grandma, who was suddenly standing by the doorway. "What do you think you're doing in there?"

Rachel emerged from the real rubbish can which she had just discovered and was searching with care.

"Looking for empty cans," she answered, startled into telling the truth. "Empty dog food cans."

"There is no need for you to do that," answered Big Grandma. "I intend to feed you, even if your sisters do not." Her eyes, one brown and one green, gleamed with amusement as she surveyed the breakfast table, and then she chuckled and rubbed her hands together.

"Isn't it lovely?" asked Phoebe, delighted with the laughter. "I did most of it."

"Then you did very well," Big Grandma replied. "Now then, put the grill on, Ruth, and make some toast. Can you make toast? Good. Rachel, wash your hands and then come and finish laying the table. Egg cups. Teacups. Milk. Sugar. Milk's in the fridge beside you. Naomi, put the kettle on. Get me a saucepan, Phoebe, from that cupboard behind you. A big one. Eggs, Naomi, don't just stand there!"

"Ordinary or horrible?" asked Naomi without thinking.

Big Grandma glanced at her. "Horrible," she replied. "Duck eggs for me, that's what I say. As many as you like. Bring them over here and pass me that box of porridge. Butter the toast, Ruth, don't let it go cold! Use your brain! Five dishes out of that cupboard, Phoebe. Egg spoons and porridge spoons, Rachel! Fill the milk jug someone! Heaven grant me patience, with milk of course! Because it's nearly empty. How you have survived so long in this hard cold world is beyond me! Tea, Naomi, four big spoonfuls and warm the pot first. In the can marked TEA! Where else would I keep it?"

In a few whirling minutes the table looked very different. Hot and bothered, the children sat down to eat. Everyone had large dishes of porridge in front of them, and Big Grandma seemed to swallow hers down before the others were even properly started.

"Hurry up!" Big Grandma encouraged them. "Shove it in, you don't need to chew porridge! Never mind if you splash it on the table, we haven't laid a cloth I see!"

Ruth and Naomi looked at each other but did not speak. Naomi was thinking that nothing would induce her to eat one of those eggs. Ruth was wondering if Rachel would choke. She could see that her sister was so flustered that she kept forgetting to take her spoon out of her mouth before she swallowed.

At last the bottoms of the bowls began to appear.

"Good-oh!" exclaimed Big Grandma without even giving them a chance to breathe.

"Toast there, here's your eggs. Who can eat two?"

"No thank you," said Ruth, Naomi, Rachel, and Phoebe all together.

"Eat them!" Big Grandma ordered. "Come on, we'll race, one for each of you and two for me. A prize for the winner!"

"What?" asked Phoebe.

"Wait and see! Eat and see!"

"You'll win," said Rachel. "It isn't worth it."

"All right, a prize for the first and second to finish. I'll say 'Go.' "

"I'm not ready," Phoebe shouted. "Someone take the top off! I can never get the tops off!"

With one swoop of the bread knife Big Grandma sliced the top off Phoebe's egg.

"Ready, steady, *go!*" she roared, and Rachel and Phoebe attacked their eggs, smashing off bits of shell with their fingers and swallowing whole.

"Finished!" they panted almost together.

"Well done!" applauded Big Grandma, clapping violently. "A prize for both of you!" She passed them each a fifty-cent piece and they beamed with delight.

"Now," she ordered, "eat up the toast. Quick, quick, before it gets cold! Marmalade on the sideboard."

Rachel and Phoebe started stuffing toast, all thoughts of dog food and Frosties forgotten.

Ruth began to shell her egg very slowly. Naomi said, "I don't usually eat breakfast."

"You'd better," Big Grandma replied, "you'll be hungry by suppertime."

"Why?" asked Naomi unguardedly.

"We're going on a picnic," Big Grandma explained.

"Well, we'll be taking food then, won't we?" asked Naomi reasonably.

"Taking food?" cried Big Grandma, gobbling toast as if she were starving. "I can't be bothered with food on a picnic! The less to carry the better. Stoke up now, while you've got the chance."

"ONE OF THE RULES of this house," Big Grandma announced when breakfast was finished and Rachel had been thumped on her back several times, "is: Those who eat least wash up."

"What do you do when you're on your own?" asked Ruth crossly.

"That," replied Big Grandma, handing her an apron and a pile of dirty plates, "you will never know."

Ruth washed and Naomi dried while Big Grandma organized the picnic. This simply meant putting a large bottle of orange squash and a few misshapen paper cups into a very shabby bag she called her knapsack.

Rachel and Phoebe, who had escaped to the garden to avoid being made to help with the breakfast things, came running back in to ask what they should take with them.

"Buckets and spades?" queried Phoebe.

But Big Grandma said no, they weren't going to the seaside. All they needed, she told them, were comfortable shoes and her trusty knapsack.

"Shall I put it in the car?" asked Rachel, wishing to seem useful, but Big Grandma replied that they would be walking not driving, and would take it in turns to carry the bag.

"Where are we going?" asked Naomi suspiciously.

"Up there," answered Big Grandma, looking out of the window toward the huge green rounded hill that rose two and a half thousand feet from sea level into the blue midsummer sky.

BIG GRANDMA'S HOUSE was built on a hillside above the village. Looking out of the front windows across the fields you saw the station, the village shop with the pub opposite, and all the houses about it, and then the sea. Far out to sea on a clear day you could see the Isle of Man, a pale blue silhouette floating on the horizon.

The picnicking expedition set off in the opposite direction to all this, across the steeply sloping field behind the house and through the Fell Gate onto the path that wound by bracken and harebells, by bilberry and heather, up to the heights where nothing grew but thin grass and lichens, and finally to where nothing grew at all, a landscape of wind and bare rock.

Some hours later Naomi collapsed onto her hands and knees and crawled the last few yards to the great cairn of flat stones that marked the summit. Rachel and Phoebe, who had arrived sometime before, were already running backward and forward with lumps of slate, intent on building a rival heap of their own.

"Look what somebody's done," called Rachel. "We're making one, too. Come and help!"

Big Grandma, apparently unaffected by the climb, opened her trusty knapsack and passed around cups of lukewarm orange squash and a small bag of extrastrong mints.

"I brought a little something," she explained kindly, "since you had so little breakfast. Take two, Naomi, most refreshing! Pass them on to Ruth, she looks quite pale!"

"I'm okay," said Ruth bravely from the slab of rock on which she had wilted. "It's just my feet and knees and back and legs and stomach and chest and head that aren't."

Big Grandma poked Naomi in the ribs with her walking stick. "You aren't enjoying yourself," she accused.

"Why did you bring us here?" asked Naomi ungratefully.

"To show you my empire," replied Big Grandma with a melodramatic flourish of her walking stick, which Rachel very luckily just managed to duck.

"It's not yours," contradicted Phoebe, as Rachel

moved prudently out of range. "What about the queen? It's hers!"

"The queen," Big Grandma told her sternly, "lives nowhere near here!"

Ruth looked around her at Big Grandma's empire, wave upon wave of purple hills inland, and a sea of silver and blue and shadowy gray shoals.

"It's very nice," she said inadequately.

"Very," agreed Naomi, thinking how swiftly her legs had changed from feeling like jelly to feeling like stone. "What do we do now?"

"Go back," answered Big Grandma airily. "What else? Stay here? Can if you like. Last one down makes supper!"

"No wonder, no wonder," cursed Ruth and Naomi as they staggered down the mountain in Big Grandma's glorious wake, "no wonder Uncle Robert ran away!"

THE FIRST DAY was nearly over. Rachel and Phoebe were helping Big Grandma wash the supper things. Try as they might they had not been able to eat as much as Ruth and Naomi, especially Naomi. Big Grandma's kitchen sink was set between two draining boards, and Big Grandma was putting washed cups and plates alternately on each board so that they could race. Rachel had already broken a saucer.

Ruth and Naomi's room, at the front of the house, shone with a gold and orange light that was pouring in through windows that faced the evening sun. Naomi was lying on her bed, finishing the last of the books that they had brought from home. Before they left they had each been allowed to choose two books, and this scheme had been a dreadful failure. The selecting of the books had been desperate work.

Phoebe had decided on an enormous coloring book, and also a story about a rabbit named Nicholas who lived, unnaturally, in a hollow tree. In spring this animal watched the flowers grow; in summer he spoke once, briefly, to a bee; in autumn he detachedly observed the falling of the leaves; and in winter, with the first deep snow, he put on striped pajamas and went to bed.

And died of boredom, thought Naomi, discarding Nicholas.

Rachel's contribution was a book of Russian folktales. Somehow, nobody had ever been able to read this book; it might have been written in the original Russian for all the progress anyone ever made. As well as this Rachel had brought a Bible, this being the only other book she owned that she had never read.

Ruth had chosen a natural history book, beautifully illustrated, but containing few words, and also a cheerful little paperback, of which they were all very fond, which dwelt, in unflinching detail, upon the nutritional habits of man-eating tigers.

In a last minute panic, Naomi had grabbed *The Treasure Seekers*. Everyone, even Phoebe, knew this book so well that they could recite whole chunks of it, but still, at least the book was rereadable. But not indefinitely. Naomi sighed, and slung it under the bed to join Nicholas. She was left with the awful choice of *Bridge for Beginners*, which she had been led to believe was an interesting game for four (if only she could understand the instructions), or plunging, straight after a large meal, into the grisly charms of the tigers.

At that moment the door was kicked open, and Ruth arrived bearing a heap of cookery books.

"All I could find," she reported, dumping them on the nearest bed. "I've looked everywhere. Big Grandma's in quite a good temper, though; she said she'd find us something better."

"As I have," remarked Big Grandma, materializing in the doorway in her usual unnerving manner. She carried three large volumes with her, and she dropped two of these on top of the cookery books.

"Let me know when you've finished them, and I'll find you something else," she said blandly, disappearing in the direction of Rachel and Phoebe's room.

"*The Annotated Shakespeare*," read Ruth and Naomi in despair. "A. L. Rowse." Naomi had the *Tragedies and Romances*, and Ruth the *Histories and Poems*. Rachel and Phoebe apparently were to get the *Comedies* to share.

"I've tried reading Shakespeare before," said Naomi. "It's impossible."

"It must be possible." Ruth did not sound very convinced. "Plenty of people do. I expect you get used to it."

"What're the cookery books like?"

Ruth inspected them critically. "Very greasy. Fingermarks all over and the covers coming off!"

"I've got to read something," Naomi said, and followed by Ruth she staggered down to the kitchen to find Big Grandma.

"Children's books?" asked Big Grandma, rolling the words like a curse. "What on earth would I be doing with children's books?"

"Well, from when Mum and, er . . ." Naomi remembered that Uncle Robert was not to be mentioned.

"Your children," supplemented Ruth hurriedly. "Any of their books from when they lived here?"

"Any your mother had worth keeping she took back for you people," said Big Grandma. "Surely you have them at home?"

"Yes, but what about Uncle Robert's?" asked Rachel tactlessly.

"Oh, Rachel," wailed her three sisters, but Big Grandma did not appear to care whether he was mentioned or not.

"I don't recall what happened to Robert's books. There couldn't have been very many. He wasn't a great reader. Most of his things went to a jumble sale, I seem to remember, and I got rid of a lot of his personal rubbish. I suppose there might have been the odd book among it."

"What sort of personal rubbish?"

"Oh, comics, papers, pictures and projects from school," said Big Grandma casually.

"How'd you get rid of it?"

"Bonfire, I expect. The usual way."

Rachel burst into tears at the thought of her own mother stirring a bonfire on which smoked all that she owned.

"She's just talking like that to be brave," whispered Ruth to Naomi.

"Who, Rachel?"

"No, Big Grandma."

They watched in silence as their brave Big Grandma mopped Rachel rather firmly with the kitchen towel.

"Children are beastly when they're overtired," remarked Big Grandma.

"So're old ladies," commented Phoebe.

Sensing that perhaps Big Grandma would resent this remark, and not wishing to be involved in any bloodshed, Ruth and Naomi vanished back to their bedroom. Phoebe stood her ground however, and was rewarded with a comradely grin from her grandmother.

"What is the matter with Rachel?" Big Grandma asked her.

"She's only gone a bit bonkers," explained Phoebe. "It doesn't matter. She often does. So do they," she jerked her head toward the staircase. "So does everyone, *I* think."

"Ah," said Big Grandma.

"Except me," said Phoebe.

"Go to bed," said Big Grandma.

Chapter 5

‹‹‹‹‹‹‹‹‹‹‹‹‹‹‹‹‹‹‹‹‹‹‹‹‹‹‹

LATE IN THE NIGHT, carrying in one hand her nightly glass of whiskey, and in the other an armload of books from her secret supply, Big Grandma climbed the stairs to bed. For a few minutes she paused outside the doors of her granddaughters' rooms, listening as they groaned in their sleep, climbing mountains in their nightmares.

Discipline is what they need, she thought as she paused on her way, discipline—Naomi stirred and moaned—fresh air and exercise—Rachel heaved a sigh that was almost a sob—a little hard work—Phoebe in her sleep turned suddenly onto her stomach and pushed her head under the pillow—and no skulking in corners reading books all day! concluded Big Grandma, and she went into her bedroom, leaving Ruth, who had suddenly jerked upright, staring into the dark with startled, still-dreaming eyes.

" 'OWING TO circumstances beyond our control,' " read Big Grandma, " 'Naomi and me cannot walk this morning. Please get a doctor.' "

Rachel and Phoebe, unlike their big sisters, had retained the use of their legs despite the mountaineering exercise of the day before, and so had been commissioned to deliver this message.

"Do your legs hurt, too?" Big Grandma asked them, honestly sorry to find that she had disabled her grandchildren on their first day with her.

"Very much," said Rachel.

"But we can still walk," added Phoebe, who was proud of this fact.

"Well, stagger back and give this to Ruth," ordered Big Grandma, scrawling, What is this I have found in my fridge? on the back of the note delivered to her, "and tell Naomi I'll be up to wash and dress her in five minutes."

The prescription worked very well. Ruth read Big Grandma's reply and suddenly remembered the large sheep's skull, complete with matching shoulder blade, that she had stuffed, inadequately wrapped in a plastic bag, beside the butter in the bottom of the refrigerator. The day before she had noticed an abundance of such relics scattered on the hillside, and had determined, in the interests of natural history, to make a collection of them.

"All such items," remarked Big Grandma, handing her a bucket when a few minutes later she hurried into the kitchen to retrieve her unlovely parcel, "are to be soaked in Clorox, dried on the lawn, and stored in the garden shed. You owe me at least a pound of butter, and you can clean the fridge after breakfast. Where's Naomi?"

"I'm here," said Naomi, who, not liking the idea of

being dressed by Big Grandma, had managed to lever her aching legs out of bed. "Don't your legs ache too?"

"Nope," said Big Grandma complacently.

"Didn't they ache the first time you went up that mountain?" persisted Naomi.

"I don't remember. I remember feeling rather tired the day I carried your mother up ..."

The girls stared at her in astonishment and disbelief.

"When she was a baby of course."

"Oh," said everyone rather flatly.

BIG GRANDMA proved to be horribly talented in finding work for other people to do. She spent the morning inventing sitting-down jobs for her guests. Every time Ruth and Naomi settled down to read a few more recipes, or Rachel and Naomi began another quarrel over the coloring book, she appeared before them, bearing a new occupation. Potatoes were scraped and lettuces washed. Dandelions were extracted from the lawn. Kitchen drawers were hauled outside for the victims to put in order.

"Quick," said Rachel, when lunch had been eaten and the dishes washed up and they had all returned to the garden. "Let's run away for a bit before she comes out with any more jobs."

"I couldn't run anywhere," said Naomi, who was recovering from the previous day much more slowly than the others, "but I don't mind if you go off without me. You could go to the village and see if that shop sells any books. Ruth could say she was going to buy more butter, that would be a good enough excuse."

"Better still just to go and not say anything at all,"

said Ruth. "I know where there's a map, I found one this morning. Anyway, we couldn't get lost, we can see the village from here, but what about you?"

"I'll be all right," said Naomi. "Buy books and magazines and comics, anything to read. And chips and chocolate. And train timetables, just in case. And ask if there's a library nearby. And see if they've got any good jigsaws. Some bananas would be nice. . . ."

Anticipating questions and objections and wishing to avoid them, the foraging party sneaked carefully around the side of the house and out into the road. Naomi watched them depart and then returned upstairs where she proceeded to arm herself with *The Annotated Shakespeare: Tragedies and Romances, Histories and Poems,* and *Comedies.*

"It's gone strangely quiet," said Big Grandma, pouncing on her as she staggered down the stairs.

"They've gone to the shop to buy that butter."

"Leaving you with nothing to do?" questioned Big Grandma. "Or perhaps not," she continued, noticing Naomi's burden. "Hoist with my own petard am I?"

"Probably," agreed Naomi, with no idea of what she was talking about. "Well, I've got all these books to read. I thought I'd take them outside."

"I suppose it will take you quite a time to get through them?" asked Big Grandma, with, Naomi thought, a wistful note in her voice.

"Hours, probably," said Naomi firmly.

BIG GRANDMA'S GARDEN was large and cheerful, usefully equipped with seats and lurking places, and edged with borders of bright flowers. The grass was very long and lumpy, not at all like the smooth green square in the garden at home. There were daisies and buttercups and dockweeds growing in it, and it was difficult to tell where the actual flower beds began because the lawn seemed to run right into them, strangling all but the most vigorous plants.

A Big Grandma-ish sort of place, thought Naomi, who long before she had finished her volumes, or indeed the first book, or in fact the first play, or, in melancholy truth, the first page, had had as much as she could bear of Shakespeare.

After Shakespeare had been discarded, and the flowers and weeds admired and dismissed, Naomi, vaguely bored and fearing that her legs would seize up again if she sat still very long, wandered off to explore the rest of the garden.

Behind the beech hedge she found fruit trees and a greenhouse containing tomato plants and shallow boxes of seedlings waiting to be planted out. Behind the greenhouse was a vegetable patch, and Naomi shuffled stiffly over to it. Peas were growing there, attached, as Naomi rightly guessed, to real pea plants (a sight she had never seen before). There were many other things, too, that Naomi did not recognize. The patch was not as weedy as the rest of the garden, and all the plants were in nice straight rows, like writing on a page. At the strawberry bed Naomi halted in amazement, for dozens of the berries sparkled there, bright red under the dark green leaves. At home they had always been the rarest of fruits, bought for Sunday dinner in summer, and eked out with ice cream. The smell of them, sweet and spicy in the warm sunshine, enticed Naomi to her knees, and there, bewitched, mesmerized, heedless of all possible consequences, she began to pick them.

Much later a blackbird screamed and broke the spell and the sun went in—not behind a cloud, but behind the huge shadow of Big Grandma. She was standing behind Naomi holding a sack and a large, shiny-pronged fork.

Naomi's life—past, present, and unthinkable future—passed in the traditional manner before her eyes. What was the sack for, she wondered, and also the very dangerous-looking fork? Could she really, as seemed only too apparent, have eaten an entire bed of strawberries? And what did Big Grandma propose to do?

"I am going to dig some potatoes for dinner," announced Big Grandma, "and I would be grateful if you would come and pick them up for me."

"I've eaten all the strawberries."

"So I see," agreed Big Grandma with no apparent emotion. "Did you enjoy them?"

"Yes, but they're all gone," said Naomi, thinking with relief that Big Grandma was probably angry, but not dangerously so. "I don't know what to do about it now."

"Potatoes," ordered Big Grandma, walking over to a patch of bushy plants. "Too late for anyone to do anything now you've eaten them. I don't see what you can possibly do about it." She stuck her fork into the ground and lifted up one of the plants. "Not at this late stage." She shook the plant and threw it aside and Naomi stared in surprise to see a number of large, pale-skinned potatoes scattered on the ground.

"You can pick them up," ordered Big Grandma, and obediently Naomi began to put them in the sack while Big Grandma stirred through the dusty earth where they had grown and uncovered more.

"Rather a groveling job." Big Grandma paused to watch Naomi scrabbling through the earth at her feet.

"Rather a dangerous-looking fork," said Naomi.

DESPITE THE FACT that from the time they left the house, Ruth, Rachel, and Phoebe could see the whole of the village, and even distinguish the particular white house that was the village shop, Ruth was determined to make full use of her map. Every time the clearly defined footpath crossed a stile or turned a corner Ruth fished out the map, laboriously located their position, and after much twisting and turning made the path marked on the map line up with the one they were following. Then she would point triumphantly in the direction in which they were to proceed. By this means they reached their destination without once getting lost.

The shop was peculiarly lacking in everything they wanted. It had no books, no comics, no toys, no chips, and no ice cream, the man said, until Thursday. He was a small, ginger-haired man, very awkward, and he stood wringing his hands and blushing redder and redder as the list of what he did not sell was revealed to them. Eventually they bought chocolate, some dreadfully expensive butter, and three very vulgar postcards (those being the only sort he sold) which Phoebe insisted upon for her schoolfriends. All the while they were making their purchases two old ladies and an ancient man scrutinized them with great care and commented freely upon their observations.

"They don't look like their mother."

"Or their poor grandmother."

"Pity."

"Aye, she were bonny in her time. Good of her to have them. More than I'd want to do."

"They look a right handful."

"They looks," said the old man loudly, "like that miserable, useless, nowt of a lad of hers!"

"Robert was a nice lad," said one old lady.

The old man examined the price of a package of crackers, snorted, and remarked, "Robbery!"

"They look like they've been poorly, all scrag, poor lasses!"

"We're not!" snapped Ruth indignantly.

"Bit of a temper, that one!"

"All the same at that age."

"Robbery!" shouted the old man, who had lost interest in the girls. "No wonder they all goes to the snooper markets!"

"Forty-seven cents isn't much," said Rachel, examining the label he was thumping with his thumb.

"Not much!" he exclaimed. "They used to be thru'pence a pound!"

"They didn't," said Phoebe belligerently. "What's 'thru'pence,' anyway? Stop poking me with them!"

Ruth, realizing that Phoebe was about to start a fight with an eighty-year-old man, shoved her out of the shop and prepared to open the map again.

"Lost already?" inquired a scruffy boy, sauntering up

the street toward them. "Straight down the road. You can see the house from here."

"She's practicing maps," explained Rachel.

"How do you know who we are?" asked Phoebe.

"Your gran said you were coming," he explained. "She said to keep an eye out for you." He was too polite to add the rest of what she had said.

"We're going to the sea," Rachel told him.

"Straight down the road the other way, then," the boy said. "You'll see the island today."

"The Isle of Man?" Ruth asked. "You can see that from Big Grandma's house. I saw it this morning."

The boy looked up at the hot blue sky and pulled his sheepskin jacket closely around him. Ruth noticed that he was wearing a thick sweater underneath. "That means rain's coming," he informed them. "When you can see the island, that means it's going to rain. And when you can't see it, that means it's raining.

"Joke," he explained as they stared blankly at him. "Oh well," he continued, giving up his hope of a laugh, "I'll be off now.

"Don't get lost," he added over his shoulder.

"He sme—" began Phoebe in a loud voice, and was stopped just in time by a hard smack from Ruth.

"What if he heard you?" Anxiously she looked after the boy, but he had not turned around. He was walking straight down the middle of the road, gazing at the world as if he owned it.

"WELL," COMMENTED NAOMI from the doorstep some time later, "I see you found the sea. Who pushed you in, Phoebe?"

"No one," answered Ruth. "She fell, running away from a wave, and it went right over her. Oh, stop whining, Phoebe, and go and put some dry clothes on. D'you know what," she continued, turning back to Naomi, "everyone knew who we were straight away!"

"We met a boy"—Rachel took up the story—"and he said Big Grandma told him to watch out for us. And it's going to rain if you see the island, and you can see it."

"You can't now," Naomi interrupted.

"You could before. Then after that we met a man who said he'd heard we were coming and he said it was a queer day and it would rain or go dark before morning, and we said how did he know, and he said it always had so far, and there were awful people in the shop, and they said . . ."

"Blow your nose, Phoebe," interrupted Naomi, bored by this recital. "What's the matter with you, anyway?"

"It's her postcards," explained Ruth. "They got soaked in the sea, and a good job, too. Show Naomi your postcards, Phoebe, and leave your ears alone."

"They've got sand in," said Phoebe, sniffing loudly and handing over her purchases.

"Nobody likes them, anyway; even the man in the shop didn't, and now they've got all wet."

"Why ever did you choose them?" Naomi eyed the postcards critically. "And why get the same picture three times?"

"The lady looks just like Big Grandma with different hair," Phoebe defended herself, "and I like sheep. There are lots of sheep around here."

"Not like these."

"Everyone knows who we are," continued Rachel, feeling that her story had been disrupted for too long, "and the old lady with the dog said she didn't know how Big Grandma was coping!"

"Anyway," said Naomi in a loud voice, "shut up a minute, Rachel. What about the books you went for? Why didn't you get any? I thought at least you'd bring back magazines or newspapers or anything."

"He doesn't sell books," Ruth told her, "and he'll only get you magazines if you order them specially and will keep on taking them for at least three months, same with newspapers. He says he doesn't want them left on his hands like he's had before."

"Well, couldn't you have bought any of the ones he'd had left on his hands, then?"

"He said he hadn't got them anymore." Ruth sighed. "I tried talking reasonably to him but he's a bit crackers and it was hard with Phoebe arguing in the background. And Rachel."

"I wasn't doing anything," put in Rachel. "Only talking quietly to myself."

"Oh, well"—Naomi rose stiffly from the doorstep—"it's suppertime. Big Grandma sent me to look for you. You'd better chuck those cards away, Phoebe, before she sees them."

"I won't!" said Phoebe indignantly. "You don't know how much they cost!"

It seemed Big Grandma was not easily shocked however, for Phoebe, recklessly ignoring her sisters' warnings, showed them to her after supper. Big Grandma admired the sheep and ironed the cards flat so that they were almost as good as new. Phoebe explained to Big Grandma her likeness to the lady in the picture, and Naomi and Ruth were surprised to find that she considered herself complimented.

"We thought you'd be cross," remarked Ruth.

"Not at my age," said Big Grandma.

IT SEEMED THAT the village weather forecasters were right in their predictions. By bedtime the sky had clouded over and the wind had dropped to the ominous trickle of a breeze that comes before a gale. In the middle of the night, Ruth was awakened by rain on her face, blown straight across the bedroom from the open window. The curtains were streaming into the room like flags, and they flapped wetly down on her as she pushed the window shut.

"About time!" came a voice from Naomi's bed. "I've been getting soaked for ages but I couldn't wake you up!"

"Why didn't you go and close it?"

"Couldn't be bothered. My legs are still stiff. Can you put the light on?"

With the window now shut they became more aware of the sounds inside. The sea wind thrummed across the chimney pots, tugged and smacked at the windowpanes, and whipped the walls with trailing branches of the ash tree that grew by the front door.

"It sounds as if the house is falling to bits," said Naomi uneasily.

"Or as if it's alive," added Ruth as at that moment the kitchen door crashed open below them, and the stairs in the sudden draught and dampness shaped their three-hundred-year-old treads and timbers to the new conditions.

"The creaks sound like coffin lids," whispered Naomi, and clutched at her knees in fear as the bathroom door slammed itself shut across the passage.

In the quietness that followed, the electric light shone cold and empty on their anxious faces.

"I'm sure this house is haunted."

"Shut up."

"Or there's someone out there."

"Shut up. Who?"

"Big Grandma?"

"She wouldn't crash around like that."

"Typical of Big Grandma," said Naomi bitterly, "to live in a haunted house!"

Although the worst of the storm had passed, the new, heavy silence was awful. Even the noise of the rain on the windows could not drown it. They dared not lie down, in case they might have to get up quickly to escape. Escape what? They did not know. Instead they dozed, sitting up, and waking with startled jerks, listening. When the rain and the wind grew louder they found themselves straining to hear above them.

There seemed to be no hope of rest or peace, and yet toward morning they fell asleep and dreamed wistfully of home.

Something very hard landed on Naomi.

Terrified she struggled with the blankets, sat up, and saw the electric lamp glowing inanely in the morning light. Phoebe was sitting on her.

"Have you any clean socks I can borrow?" she asked.

"You nearly gave me a heart attack!" Naomi shoved her onto the floor. "And no I haven't. Anyway, mine would be too big for you."

"I often wear your socks," said Phoebe incautiously.

"Well, you're not doing it this time." Naomi returned happily to the world of scrounging sisters and petty theft. "Go and pinch some of Ruth's before she wakes up."

Two slates had fallen off the roof in the night, wrenched away by the wind. One of them slithered to the ground and smashed on the front doorstep exactly where Naomi had been sitting the day before. It rained all day, not hard, but continuously. Big Grandma hardly took any notice of the weather at all. She spent the afternoon in a deck chair in the greenhouse, peacefully writing letters, and seemed surprised, on returning to the house, to find that nobody else had been out. The washing from the day before hung on the line so heavy with rain that it would have sagged to the ground if it hadn't been sustained by the clothes prop in the middle. "You'd think one of us would have had the wits to bring it in," remarked Big Grandma, but she did not seem particularly distressed.

Nobody but Ruth and Naomi seemed to have been disturbed by the noises of the night. Not wishing to make fools of themselves, they did not mention their uneasy night to anyone, but privately, in their bedroom, they discussed the matter.

"You said this house was haunted."

"You didn't say it wasn't."

Later on they both spent some time slamming doors

and running up and down the stairs, endeavoring to recreate the sounds of the night, until ordered to desist by Big Grandma, on pain of being given something productive to do. In the darkest parts of their minds they both believed, not entirely unwillingly, that the house was haunted. Naomi appropriated Rachel's Bible, and Ruth noticed that she took it to bed with her that evening.

"What's that for?" she asked crossly. "To throw at the ghost?"

"Yes," said Naomi unreassuringly, although she did not need it after all. They were haunted by nothing worse than a looting party, led by Phoebe in the early hours of the morning.

"How come they've got so many?" whispered Rachel from the doorway.

"They never change them, that's why," answered Phoebe, tiptoeing away with her arms full of socks.

THE RAIN did not stop after one day as everyone had hoped it would. It went on and on and there was nothing to do. No secret passages were discovered, and they tapped in vain upon the walls of the house, listening for a "hollow sound." Big Grandma explained quite kindly to them that although the walls were two feet thick, they were solid stone right through. ("Except for the garage," she added, "which is a twentieth-century breeze-block atrocity, but serves its purpose.") So they abandoned the walls, and decided to hunt for trapdoors in the floors instead, and Naomi had quite a nice time organizing Rachel and Phoebe onto their knees in the attic, listening for suspicious squeaking boards. Ruth came up and spoiled it.

"Trapdoors in the attic will go into the bedrooms and trapdoors in the bedrooms will go into the living rooms and trapdoors in them go to the coal cellar and the coal cellar floor is just the hillside, you know it is; you can see where the rock shows through!"

"Oh, go away," said Naomi peevishly.

To Big Grandma the days of wet weather seemed like a time of constant searching, as the girls wandered preoccupied through the house, questing for ghosts, books, relics of the mysterious disappearing Uncle Robert, secret passages, something to do, books, books, books, anything to read. A less determined woman would have broken down, but Big Grandma did not.

TOWARD THE END of the week, as the supply of unread cookery books dwindled, as the rain continued to pour, and as people became less and less tolerant of their relations' little imperfections of character, the strain began to show. Rachel and Phoebe staged a spectacular fight which began at the top of the stairs and ended when they rolled in a heap at their grandmother's feet in the hall below, still gripping handfuls of each other's hair, after having smashed a banister on the way down.

"She blew at me," raged Phoebe as Big Grandma ripped them apart.

"I can blow at whoever I like!" screeched Rachel, lunging at her sister. Big Grandma locked them in the dining room to fight it out and for quite a long time there was no sound to be heard from them but that of loud blowing and running footsteps. When the room grew quiet and Big Grandma cautiously opened the door they were both fast asleep on the hearthrug, exhausted by the struggle.

Ruth wandered around the house, depressed not only by the general gloom, but also because to date her collection of interesting bones consisted of one skull and one shoulder blade. On top of this, she still had no proof that the house was haunted, although she lay awake and heard prowling ghosts for several hours every night. Naomi refused to discuss the matter, finding even the idea intolerable. She no longer had much faith in the deterrent powers of Rachel's Bible, for encountering Big Grandma unexpectedly on a midnight visit to the bathroom, and mistaking her in the dark for an unearthly apparition, she had thrown the Bible with great presence of mind (and force) into Big Grandma's stomach.

"If I had been what you thought I was," said Big Grandma nastily when she had undoubled, "that would have gone straight through me and you would have died of shock!"

What upset Naomi most, however, was that the Bible had ripped apart, the pages torn away from the hard cover. She was sure a Bible in two pieces would not work.

"Go away," said Big Grandma one morning, in her usual unfeeling way. "Go out. I cannot bear you any longer. I didn't invite you here so that you might spend the whole summer breathing your quarrelsome little breaths down my neck." And she forced them to put on coats, fitted them out with umbrellas, and pushed them out for a walk. They slopped sulkily down to the post office and bought stamps and candy.

"Ice cream's here," said the shopman proudly. "Told you we'd be getting it in!" He wrung his hands and grinned weakly at them and pointed to a colored chart which displayed the different ice creams and Popsicles he had now acquired.

"They'd wash away if we took them outside," Ruth said.

The shopman straightened up and looked indignantly at her. "Better not grumble, had we? Rain's what makes the lakes, and the lakes are what the visitors come for."

They stumped back up the hill feeling snubbed.

"You're back quickly," said Big Grandma as they came in. "Out you go again!" and before they could protest she had handed Rachel a bundle of letters to mail, and shut the front door on them.

"What shall we do?" asked Rachel, looking at the letters as if they might explode.

"Mail them," said Ruth, "or she'll never let us in again."

"Drop them," ordered Naomi, and Rachel, who had been trained to obey, dropped them in the mud.

"Now pick them up," said Naomi, "and come on, or we'll be out all night."

"Why did Rachel have to drop them?" asked Phoebe, running after her as she set off down to the village again.

"She was watching from the window," explained Ruth, "smirking!"

"Self-defense," added Naomi. "After all, she attacked first!"

Chapter 6

ONCE, MUCH EARLIER in the history of the Conroy family, a colored pamphlet had arrived at the house through the mail. It had been found by Rachel, and Rachel had kept it a secret. As far as she could make out it was offering free books (there had been a picture of the books) to anyone who cared to tick off the ones they wanted and mail it back with their name and address filled in where it said NAME and ADDRESS. Rachel had carried out these instructions, and for a long time, even when the twenty-four very heavy books had been returned, she had received letters addressed to "Dear Sir/Madam." The books were almost forgotten now, and so was the cost of their return postage, and even the threats of what would happen to her if she ever did such a thing again. All that remained in Rachel's memory of the incident was the knowledge that you could begin a letter "Dear Sir/Madam," and it would do for anyone in the world.

"Dear Sir/Madam," wrote Rachel to her parents,

The sausages here are not like the sausages at home they are all one long one that you have a bit of. We had sausages for supper. Ruth is writing to you and so is Naomi and so is Phoebe. We are having a nice time. ["That's a lie," Naomi said, reading over Rachel's shoulder.]

Love from Rachel

Do you miss me?

Phoebe's letter was very short and she would not accept any help with the spelling so no one knew what it was about. She wrote it lying on the floor with the paper shoved under her stomach, and after a long and painful time she had accomplished one line which simply remarked: "I hop you will send my muny son."

The rest of the page she filled with kisses, and she drew a picture of money on the back.

After a lot of staring at the ceiling Ruth began:

Dear Mum and Dad,

I hope you are well. I will have to buy another suitcase to put my bones in. I do not know how much they cost. I don't know what Phoebe is writing—she will not show anyone. Please could you send us some books to read. We have read all of Big Grandma's and there is no library in the village. Please send as many as you can—it doesn't matter which. We climbed a huge mountain the day Mum went away and the next day we went to the beach, but it has done nothing but rain since. Big Grandma makes us go out even if it is raining because she doesn't want us under her feet all day. We have been doing all the work, and washing up after every meal (unless we eat until we are nearly sick like she does). Big Grandma says there are badgers living near here. I'm going to see them if it stops raining. Sometimes (but not often) she is quite nice to us. I hope the books come soon.

Love Ruth

P.S. There are a lot of things I would like to say but am not saying, so this is a rather short letter.

Naomi wrote:

Dear Everyone,

Will you write and tell us when we are coming home so I can count the days off? Every day Big Grandma forces us out in the rain and we have to go and stand in the shed until she lets us in again. She thinks we go for walks, but she cannot make us. We have not got anything to read, but we have to work all day so we do not have much spare time. We talk about Robert in front of Big Grandma—she doesn't care. She says she doesn't believe in living in the past—she says you do. One of us has been stealing stuff from the garden, two people (or it might be three) have been stealing my socks, one of us is wearing nearly the same clothes that they wore when we came here. They have not worn anything else in-between. Two of us have learned foul language off someone (me and one of us knew it already but at least we did not use it). Do you think we sound like we are getting worse? I heard Big Grandma tell you on the phone that we were all well. Well, some of us could hardly walk that day.

Love Naomi.

P.S. I hope you enjoy spending all that money.

P.P.S. I do not mean to sound nasty.

Chapter 7

"BEASTLY BORING to you!" sang Rachel to the tune of "Happy Birthday." "Beastly boring to you, beastly boring, beastly boring, beastly boring to you!"

"When is it going to stop raining?" asked Phoebe.

"Never," said Naomi.

In this, as in so many other matters, she proved to be wrong. After four days of pouring rain they awoke one morning to a world of bright sunlight. Everyone's spirits rose tremendously at this transformation, and Ruth, looking out of the window, voiced all their hopes when she said, "Perhaps the washing will dry today."

They had reached the stage when everyone's clothes were equally dirty, and even Phoebe had taken to wearing her own again.

The sunshine went straight to Big Grandma's head. In celebration of the weather she cooked them fried egg sandwiches for breakfast, and sang, as she slapped the eggs onto the bits of bread, French words to a tune so eerie, so desolate and disturbing, that the hairs curled on the back of Ruth's neck as she listened.

"What's that song?" she inquired.

" 'Lili Marlene,' " answered Big Grandma and swopped over to the English words.

"It is awful," said Ruth admiringly, and was disappointed when Big Grandma refused to continue.

"Nobody could sing with Rachel eating fried egg sandwiches only feet away," she said in excuse. Rachel, who with complete lack of foresight, had just taken a large and disastrous bite into the middle of her sandwich, smiled unconcernedly and licked the front of her T-shirt.

"How poor Noah," said Big Grandma, "survived forty days cooped up with his relations in that ark is past my understanding."

"He probably had plenty of books with him," said Naomi.

"And he could always go and sit with the animals," pointed out Ruth.

"True," agreed Big Grandma, "and speaking of animals, you lot of gorging gluttons have eaten me out of house and home. What will I do with you while I go shopping?"

"Why don't you take us with you?" asked Rachel.

"Why should I?" asked Big Grandma reasonably. "Much quicker and less embarrassing without you, I should think. But what will my poor little grandchildren do without their Big Grandma all day, especially as I intend locking them out of the house?"

"Well, we'll smash a window and come back in," said Phoebe in a moment of inspiration.

"Oh really?" asked Big Grandma. "It's not that easy to smash a window in cold blood, my sweet little Phoebe!"

"Why not?"

"Try it and see," said Big Grandma, and smirked complacently after Rachel had rushed outside, grabbed a large stone, and then, to her surprise, been unable to do more than grin weakly and slink back in again.

"Mind over matter," explained Big Grandma arrogantly.

At that moment Phoebe, who had been carefully selecting a likely looking missile, turned and chucked it through the kitchen window where it smashed a neat, but rather large hole in the dead center.

"Matter over mind," said Naomi. "Quite a good shot, too!"

"It's easy," explained Phoebe modestly, coming in to view the damage from the other side.

"You horrible child," snarled Big Grandma. "I should never have judged you by human standards! Witless! Leave that glass alone, Rachel, you'll cut yourself! And you two stop laughing," she ordered Ruth and Naomi. "Get on with the dishes while I clear this mess up."

"Who—me?" asked Ruth, enraged. "I ate two eggs!"

"You said I could," Phoebe complained, disappointed at not being praised for her achievement.

"Can you glue it together with see-through glue?" asked Rachel, without much hope.

"Are you still locking us out all day?" asked Naomi, wondering if brute force had caused Big Grandma to change her mind.

"I certainly am," said Big Grandma crossly, "and you'll be lucky if I don't leave you outside all night as well."

"Can we have some food if you do?" asked Rachel,

who wisely believed her Big Grandma to be capable of anything. "And sheets and blankets and pillows and candles and our pajamas, and umbrellas in case it rains?"

"I'll see how I feel," replied Big Grandma as she wrapped up pieces of broken glass in newspaper. "You might not even survive till night. What are you going to do all day? Have you an idea between you?"

"If we're going to be out all day," suggested Ruth, "we could make a fire and cook our dinner on it. We don't like sandwiches."

"Do you know how?" asked Big Grandma. "Have you ever done it before?"

"You learn it in the Guides," replied Ruth cautiously, and none of her sisters gave her away by pointing out that she had been thrown out of that noble institution after only two weeks' membership, on a charge of non-cooperation.

"It's perfectly easy," added Naomi. "Dozens of books tell you how to do it, and anyway, we've been reading cookery books all week."

"I suppose I could let you do it if you did it on the beach," Big Grandma said. "There's nothing to set fire to down there. I don't see why you shouldn't manage. Keep Phoebe and Rachel away from the flames though, and don't forget everything you need you'll have to carry down yourselves, and you can thank Phoebe for that. I haven't time to take you as well as get this window patched up."

"Oh, there won't be much to carry," said Ruth.

AN HOUR LATER they set off for the beach completely bowed down under the weight of their equipment. Not only had they food, in vast and bulky quantities, but also a saucepan, a frying pan, half a gallon of fresh water, and a bucket to be filled with sea water and stood near the fire, just in case.

"Don't you trust us?" asked Naomi, when Big Grandma produced this.

"Not entirely," said Big Grandma.

As well as all this they took newspaper to help get the fire started, swimming things in case they went swimming, and an assorted bundle of knives and forks. Ruth, very alarmed already at the size of the heap on the kitchen floor, said she thought they could do without plates.

"What about a table and a few chairs?" asked Big Grandma when she saw the stack of essential equipment, "or perhaps you could choke down sandwiches just this once?"

This was exactly what they had been thinking themselves, but nobody had any intention of saying so. Between them they shouldered the load and headed off for the shore, trying to walk as if their backs and arms were not breaking because Big Grandma was standing at the front door, gleefully watching and waving good-bye.

All through the village people stared at them.

"Haven't they ever seen anyone carrying a frying pan before?" muttered Naomi.

"It's Phoebe's bucket," grumbled Ruth. Phoebe was carrying (among other things) an orange plastic bucket half full of apples and tomatoes. Unable to lift it properly, she was trailing it along the ground behind her, the apples and tomatoes bumping and rattling about inside. At the village shop they stopped to buy fizzy pop, and they put that in the bucket as well.

"It's too heavy," complained Phoebe.

"I'll take it, then," said Naomi, "and you take this blasted awful frying pan."

Phoebe, already burdened by a small sack of potatoes held strained to her chest by her aching arms, found that the addition of a frying pan obscured her vision completely.

"Stop dragging it," ordered Ruth, a few minutes later, when Phoebe had resorted to towing the frying pan along the road behind her. "It'll get scratched. Carry it properly. You've destroyed enough for one day."

The road led through the village, past fields of sheep on either side, and down to the very edge of the beach. Few people visited this part of the coast, mainly because there was nowhere to park a car, and none of the usual seaside souvenir shops. Instead the salt-scorched grass sloped down to the shore and ended in an expanse of rough stone and shingle. When the tide was up you could not see any sand at all, but when it was down it left a shining flatness of golden beach, stranded shells, and rock pools.

"Gosh!" said Naomi, gazing in delight over the rim of her bucket, "why didn't you tell me it was this good?"

The tide was out, and in the far distance the sea sparkled along the edge of the sand. Except for a few groups of people sitting on the stones just in front of where the road ended, the beach was empty.

"Let's get away from them," said Ruth, looking at the people. "We'll go where no one can see what we're doing if anything goes wrong."

They trudged a long way before Ruth and Naomi were satisfied with the distance between themselves and the rest of the world.

"My feet are bleeding," said Rachel sadly. "My socks are full of blood. I can feel it squidging between my toes. Can't we stop?"

Heartlessly Ruth and Naomi hurried on, until the people on the beach disappeared into the blur of the heat haze.

"Should be safe here," said Ruth at last, dumping her burdens to the ground. "It'll be lighter going back when we've eaten all the food," she added thankfully, for the pile on the shore looked even bigger than it had done on the kitchen floor.

"I can't walk," said Rachel, collapsing on the wet sand. "You'll have to carry me down to the sea."

Already her sisters were pulling on their swimsuits.

"Come on," said Ruth to Rachel, "you'll feel better when you've got your shoes off."

"I'm sure my socks are full of blood."

"Let's see, then," said Naomi.

Rachel slowly pulled off her socks while her sisters stared at her bare feet in silence.

"It's disgusting!"

"Get them away from the food!"

"Blood?" asked Phoebe in amazement. "That's not blood! Blood's not black! That's—"

"Shut up," Ruth told her. "We all know what it is."

"Aren't you sorry for me?" asked Rachel, shamelessly regarding her feet, but instead of answering her the same thought struck all her sisters at once, and they rushed to get into the sea before Rachel, as Naomi put it, mucked it up.

Ruth and Naomi had read between them a fair number of books describing how to make a campfire, and they had noticed that most of them seemed concerned to point out the enormous problems of the business, laying great stress on the need to identify the sorts of wood that burned best, the troubles that could arise when the wind blew in the wrong direction, the special skills required to build a fireproof circle of stones, and the best (and only) way to sharpen a stick on which to spear your food.

"I'm sure they write like that to put people off trying," decided Naomi, who regarded these accounts as pure fiction. Cooking on a sharpened stick she unsportingly dismissed as impossible, and as for the building of the fireplace, well, any fool could make a circle of stones, especially if they were lucky enough to have someone else to do the carrying for them. In this respect Ruth and Naomi were very lucky, since they had Rachel and Phoebe.

"We need two more," dictated Naomi, "long, flattish ones to balance the saucepan and the frying pan on."

"Big Grandma said we weren't to go near the fire," Phoebe pointed out.

"She meant when it was alight, not now," said Ruth, who was arranging the stones. "Anyway, you don't usually do what she tells you. Go and get some dried seaweed, there's heaps of it piled farther up the beach."

The stones were arranged in a neat circle in the sand, with screwed-up newspaper in the middle and sticks and seaweed on top. With immense care they lit the newspaper, and the campfire burned with flames that were almost invisible in the bright sunlight.

"One match," said Ruth proudly, "and Big Grandma made me bring two boxes!"

Rachel and Phoebe were sent off to the sea with the bucket to wash the potatoes, which were then cut up (unpeeled) and put in the saucepan.

"We forgot the salt," said Naomi.

"The sea is salt," answered Ruth. "And boiling will kill the germs. Go and rinse the bucket, Rachel, and get us a bit of sea. A clean bit. Don't get it from where you were paddling!"

"Stand on the edge and get it," said Ruth. "Don't put your feet in."

While the potatoes boiled in a mixture of salt and fresh water on one side of the fire Naomi fried bacon on the other, holding the pan as far away from herself as possible because the flames were so hot.

"Shall we fry the tomatoes too?" asked Ruth, feeding the fire with the bits of driftwood Rachel and Phoebe were collecting.

"They'd be much cooler raw," decided Naomi, feeling she had quite enough to manage with the bacon alone.

"This cooking is dead easy." Ruth prodded the potatoes. "I knew it would be. These are soft enough to eat now. What about the bacon?"

"I've cooked it all. Smell it. I wish you could get perfume that smelled that way."

"What way?"

"Fried bacon. Call Rachel and Phoebe and let's get started. I'm starving!"

"G O O D J O B there isn't any gravy," commented Ruth, looking across at Rachel. Rachel was holding a slice of bacon in one hand and a large potato speared on a fork in the other. Tomato juice ran unconfined along her forearm and dripped off her elbow.

"It's jolly good," said Rachel happily. "I didn't know we could cook."

"You didn't cook," Naomi pointed out. "Ruth and I cooked. You did all the work, but we were the brains. Chuck me another tomato someone! *Someone* not *everyone!*"

"Is it the one who eats least washes up?" asked Phoebe, "or the one who finishes last?"

"Neither," said Ruth indignantly, reaching over to pick another slice of bacon from the frying pan and spitting out potato skins. "We're not at Big Grandma's now! This is civilization! Have you forgotten what it's like?"

T H E R E W A S a happy feeling in the air, a feeling of slowly regained control. It seemed a very long time since they had felt so peaceful. Home, school, the monotonous struggle to retain their flawed, familiar, and uncompromising characters in a blandly civilizing world, even the fortunes they had gained and lost so quickly all seemed very far away. Here they were, not starving or food-poisoned, doing what they had set out to do and doing it well.

Fate, in the form of a stocky, sheepskin-jacketed individual, was already scurrying toward them, but of that they were happily unaware.

GRAHAM, LOOKING across the fields of his father's farm to the sea, saw that some daft holiday-maker had lit a fire, and being the son, grandson, and great-grandson of Cumbrian farmers, he had been brought up to regard all holiday-makers with great suspicion. Very early in his life he had been taught the holiday-maker rules. He knew, for instance, that if they walked through a field you should go after them and check the gates. That their picnic spots must be constantly patrolled and their dangerous rubbish removed. It was to be expected that they would park their cars in gateways, feed your horse with sandwiches, and lose their dogs in fields of sheep. And although they rarely meant any harm—the majority of them treasuring the countryside as much as any farmer (but Graham could never have believed that)—they must always be watched. In case.

It was not the remains of a successful dinner party that Graham saw on the beach. He saw smoke, and a great heap of goodness knew what, and reckless people mucking about poking the fire with long sticks. He heard wild and awful singing and he did not know that it was only Ruth, teaching her sisters the words of "Lili Marlene." He drew closer, slightly shocked, and realized that it was not any old mad holiday-makers, but those grandchildren of Mrs. Sayers on the hill, and he knew for a fact that they were weak in the head, because she had told him so herself.

Remembering this he lost no time in running across the field, hauling himself over the wall that kept the sheep from straying onto the beach, scrambling over the rocks, and completely spoiling the campfire by emptying the orange plastic bucket of seawater right in the middle of it.

"You shouldn't be mucking about with fires!" he told his flabbergasted audience through the thick smoke that was now billowing around them. "Not unless you've got someone responsible with you! I'd have thought your gran would have had more sense than to let you!"

"It's that boy," said Ruth, as she struggled to hold Phoebe back, "that boy we saw the other day. Don't you dare, Phoebe!"

"The one that said it would rain," added Rachel, as if the rain had been all his fault.

"The one that I said smelled and you hit me," supplemented Phoebe, wriggling free from Ruth's grip. "All right, I'm not going to do anything to him!"

"He seems somewhat lacking," remarked Naomi, recalling a favorite phrase of Big Grandma's.

"What do you think you're doing, then?" asked Graham, considerably unnerved to find he was surrounded by a circle of half-dressed, wholly threatening females, at least two of them as tall, if not taller than himself. There seemed to be every possibility that he would have to fight his way out.

One of the girls, the least skinny and ferocious looking, said (in a very pleased voice), "Look, he's going to cry!"

"Him cry?" asked another. "Him cry? It's us that should be crying!"

The smallest, and most dreadfully threatening of them all said, "He's only little. Do you want me to fight him?"

"Little yourself," replied Graham defiantly. "I'm older than you lot!"

"How d'you know?"

"Your gran told me. She told me all about you before you came here."

"Why did she tell you about us?"

"Why shouldn't she?" asked Graham unwisely. "She told a lot of folk. Everyone knew you were coming."

The eldest two glanced at each other and then reseated themselves, inviting him, rather earnestly, to tell them what else Big Grandma had said. Rachel, suddenly spotting a tomato that had been overlooked earlier, settled down to consume it, and Graham, seeing that he must either sit down, too, or remain confronting Phoebe alone, squatted uncomfortably beside the wet ruins of the bonfire.

The conversation got off to a bad start.

"What's your name?"

"What's it to you?"

"Well, we've got to call you something. We'll call you Emily, then. Did Big Grandma tell you our names, Emily?"

"You give up calling me that!"

"What's your name then?"

"Graham."

"That's Rachel," said one of the girls, nodding to the one who had said he was going to cry. "I'm Naomi. That's Ruth. That one walking around you holding her nose is Phoebe. . . ."

"That's never her real name, is it?" asked Graham, shocked.

Phoebe, who had endured this question in various forms all her life, pulled a dreadful face and choked, as if overcome by fumes.

"Take no notice," said Ruth civilly. "She hasn't had a bath for a week."

"I had one last night," remarked Graham, cheering up a bit at this information.

"Did Big Grandma tell you we were horrible?" asked Rachel.

"She didn't say anything nasty about you like that."

"She must have said something. Why did you come tearing down here?"

"I saw you playing with the fire and I came to stop you before you got into trouble."

"Why should we?"

Graham shrugged. "What she said about you."

"What?"

"She said you were weak in the head," said Graham, throwing tact and caution to the winds. "She said you weren't fit to be let out hardly."

There was silence. Phoebe let go of her nose and looked at Ruth and Naomi for guidance, not knowing who was attacking whom anymore. Cautiously she edged behind Graham and stuck her tongue out.

"Huh," said Naomi eventually.

"Well," said Ruth, pulling herself together, "d'you believe everything you hear? Look at our fire! Look at our towels! Lucky we'd finished our cooking, that's all!"

"Lucky for *him*!" remarked Phoebe.

"She said you have no manners," remarked Graham, dispassionately.

"What, all of us, or just Phoebe?" demanded Rachel.

"Yes," Ruth had to agree with this logic, "yes, well, Phoebe hasn't got any manners, it's true. Neither has Rachel," she admitted honestly. "Probably they're not really fit to be let out! Shut up, Rachel! But me and Naomi are looking after them. . . ."

"How d'you do that, then?" asked Graham, looking at Rachel and Phoebe as if they were some unusual form of livestock.

"Bribery mostly," Naomi told him.

Graham looked blank, so Ruth and Naomi proceeded to demonstrate.

"You two go off and fill that bucket with seawater and rinse the knives and stuff in it," ordered Naomi, "and we'll wash up tonight when we get back."

Rachel, who was trying to think of a way of proving she had manners without being rude, took no notice. Phoebe raised one eyebrow.

"And we'll set the table for supper as well."

Phoebe's eyebrow lowered fractionally and Rachel looked up.

"And we won't make you carry any of this cooking stuff back when we go."

"Promise?"

"Promise."

"Promise on Big Grandma's deathbed?" said Rachel suspiciously.

"Oh, all right."

Convinced by this awful oath, Rachel and Phoebe set

off with the bucket, leaving Ruth and Naomi regarding Graham cautiously, wondering if he was impressed, what else he knew, and if he had any books that he might lend them.

"How d'you know Big Grandma?" asked Ruth at last. "Do you go up to the house ever?"

"I go to help in the garden now and then. Why?"

"Well, do you know anything about it?"

"What she means is," Naomi put in, "is it haunted?"

"Might be," replied Graham. "Lots of places around here are."

"Where?"

"Churchyard."

"Is that haunted?"

"Bound to be," said Graham, who hated conversations like this. "All those corpses! Bound to be . . . Is that what you told them to do?" he added, looking toward Rachel and Phoebe on the water's edge, and then getting hastily to his feet as he saw them hurl the last of the knives in the bucket and start back to rejoin the party.

"Yes," said Naomi complacently, "told you we could manage them."

"You got a lot of work to put in yet," commented Graham. "Anyway, I've got to be off. Tell your gran I'll be coming up to your place with the eggs tomorrow."

"Bother," said Ruth looking after him as he hurried away. "I wanted to ask if he'd lend us some books. Look at him! Almost running! It's Phoebe's fault! I know Rachel's pretty awful too. . . ."

"I'm not!" said Rachel, overhearing this last remark.

"But Phoebe's awful on purpose!"

"Why shouldn't I be?" asked Phoebe cheerfully.

RUTH HAD a brilliant idea when it came to packing up to go home.

"We're bound to want this stuff again," she pointed out. "We'll leave it here. We can't keep carrying it up and down with us."

"Somebody will steal it or it will wash away," said Naomi.

"Not if we bury it!"

"Big Grandma will kill you," remarked Rachel, but was overruled by the majority. Using the knives and the frying pan they dug a deep hole under the rocky bank that Graham had slid down to save their lives. The knives and smaller things went into the bucket, and they left the saucepan handle sticking out to mark the spot when they came to dig them up again.

"Better bring back Big Grandma's knapsack," said Naomi. "She'll go mad if we bury it."

"She'll go mad, anyway," said Rachel with prophetic gloom.

IT DID NOT TAKE long for Big Grandma to spot the empty rucksack and make her attack.

"What have you done with everything?" she demanded.

"They buried it," said Rachel, who wanted no part in the matter.

"Half wits!" stormed Big Grandma. "Go back and dig it up again!"

"We're fed up with you calling us names," said Naomi resentfully. "You told everyone in the village we weren't fit to be let out!"

"Well, you're not," snapped Big Grandma. "Look at you! Buried it! I've a good mind to make you go back and fetch everything right now! I would too if it weren't suppertime. I don't suppose you've had anything to eat all day. Did you bury the food as well?"

"We ate it," said Rachel. "Me and Phoebe cooked it and it was lovely. We'll cook some for you tomorrow if you like." She yawned. "Perhaps."

"Did you have the sense to mark the place?" asked Big Grandma.

"Yes," answered everyone, thinking of the saucepan handle sticking up out of the sand.

"Well," said Big Grandma, dropping poached eggs onto slices of toast with such force that they burst on impact, "well, it had better be there in the morning. Or else."

"Or else what?" asked Phoebe.

"Or else you'll be sorry," said Big Grandma.

Chapter 8

◄◄◄◄◄◄◄◄◄◄◄◄◄◄◄◄◄◄◄◄◄◄◄◄

POSTCARDS ARRIVED for the girls the next morning, one each (to avoid quarrels), but all sent in the same brown envelope, so as not to waste stamps. Mrs. Conroy wrote to Rachel:

Rachel Darling,

Thank you for your nice letter. You *know* you change your clothes every day, don't you, except for sweaters and big things. And pajamas every three or four days perhaps. And take the grubby ones down for Grandma to wash. Yes, we do miss you, very much!

Lots of love, Mummy and Daddy

and she wrote:

Hello Phoebe!

You will have to get someone to help you read this.
Thank you for your letter. We wondered what the
picture was, but your writing is getting nice and
neat. Hope you are being *very good*! Of course you
are! Ask Rachel to show you her postcard.

Bye bye sweetheart, Mum and Dad
XXX

Naomi's was rather more terse:

Naomi! What a letter! I'm sure you *did* mean to
sound nasty! Hope the weather is better and you
have cheered up again. Do make sure the Little
Ones change their clothes, if Grandma does not
notice. She says you have been quite good, so
perhaps a lot of your letter was exaggerated! I hope
so! Write us a nice one!

Love and kisses, Mum and Dad

Ruth read:

Dear Ruth,

Daddy and I did laugh at your letter! A suitcase for
your bones! I'm sure you haven't read all
Grandma's books! Anyway, books are far too
heavy to send! Do help Rachel and Phoebe about

clothes, etc. I have said the same to Naomi. Glad to hear you are helping so much.

Love and kisses, Mum and Dad

"She's not sending any books." Ruth passed her card over to Naomi and took Rachel's to read.

"She seems worried about your clothes," commented Big Grandma, "which is not surprising. Still, you all know where the laundry hamper is, so I shall leave what you wear to your own consciences."

"Our clothes are all the same," said Ruth, "clean and awful or dirty and awful. Show me your postcard, Naomi."

"S'private," said Naomi.

"So is mine," Rachel remarked, "but you all went and read it."

"Because we knew you had nothing to hide," Big Grandma told her.

Phoebe listened in silence while her postcard was read aloud to her, and later, while the others were washing up, she inspected the correspondence again, and carefully turned the brown paper envelope inside out. Eventually she was forced to conclude that her parents had once again forgotten to hand over her money. How they could forget, Phoebe found difficult to imagine. She remembered it all the time. She sought out Naomi for advice.

"What d'you think has happened to it?"

Naomi was inspecting a pair of shears in the garden shed, snapping the blades together with a professional air.

"Stand still while I see if these are sharp enough."

Phoebe obligingly stood still while Naomi sheared off a few curls.

"Sharp as sharp," Naomi said. "They've prob'ly spent it."

"'Course they haven't. Give me a turn."

Naomi handed over the shears and turned her back. "Only a bit then, like I chopped off you."

"I can't reach. Bend down."

Naomi bent down and Phoebe sliced off an extremely large hunk of her hair.

"Oh!" exclaimed Naomi, grabbing the handful as it fell. "That's ten times what I chopped off you."

"My hand slipped."

"Well, you've got to give me another turn to make it fair. Stand still in case I slice your ears."

Phoebe clutched her ears in delicious horror while Naomi opened the shears to their widest extent and then snapped them suddenly shut as she glimpsed Big Grandma coming down the garden path.

"Have you done it?" Phoebe let go of her ears and opened her eyes.

"No. Buzz off quick. Here's Big Grandma!"

Phoebe buzzed off by way of the broad-bean rows, while Naomi hastily stuffed strands of hair into a bag of potting compost and tried not to look guilty. She always felt guilty when she met Big Grandma in the garden. Big Grandma had a hold over Naomi, and she had it because Naomi had eaten all the strawberries. Like a criminal returning to the scene of the crime, Naomi would wander down to the vegetable garden and stare at the plundered plants, willing more berries to grow and ripen. They never did. It was the end of the season for strawberries; those had been the very last. Always after Naomi had stared at the strawberry bed her attention would be caught by others things: raspberries and loganberries, peapods and radishes. And then Big Grandma would appear from nowhere and, whether Naomi was guilty or not, she always felt herself turning a bright, incriminating red.

Big Grandma never said, "You ate the strawberries and trampled the plants into the ground." She never exclaimed, "Caught you at it!" when she came across Naomi with her mouth full of raw carrot, or in the act of sampling the red currants. What she would say was, "I wish I could get my parsley weeded," or, "How about raking all those potato tops together and putting them on the compost heap?" and Naomi would find herself in for another spot of hard labor.

THIS TIME Big Grandma merely remarked that the edges of the lawn needed clipping and that she had two dozen young lettuces in the greenhouse that needed planting before they got too big.

Naomi received this information without flinching, and by the time Ruth found her half an hour later she was already hard at work, meeting Big Grandma's challenge.

"Aren't you coming with us?" asked Ruth. "We're going swimming and making sure that stuff is still where we left it."

"I'm doing this," replied Naomi, clipping and clipping

on her aching knees. "Oh, damn these horrible shears. They're all the wrong shape!"

"What's wrong with them?"

"They twist my wrists. If you see that boy again, you know, what's his name? Graham. Ask if he'll lend us some books."

"Why don't you come with us? You don't really have to do that. We're going to get ice cream at the shop."

"Yes, you leave it if you want to," Big Grandma called, overhearing them.

"I'm doing it," replied Naomi crossly. "I don't want to go to the rotten beach, anyway," and she turned her back on them and continued to hack off chunks of stiff grass, all mixed up with dandelions and weeds. Disturbed ants crawled over her hands, and once she chopped a big fat slug into two soggy halves before she noticed it.

"When did you last do this?" she asked Big Grandma.

"Ages ago."

The morning slipped away.

"Stop if you want to," dared Big Grandma.

"I said I'd do it," Naomi answered. "I'll plant the lettuces when I've finished this."

"I could do them myself," threatened Big Grandma. "Now, if you like."

"I like planting things," said Naomi grimly.

PHOEBE AND RACHEL bought plastic, seaside spades at the shop, but the handle of Phoebe's snapped off in the first ten minutes of digging. Over and over again one or another of them would go back to the end of the road, and carefully pace along the beach the distance they thought they had gone the day before, and then they would search that patch for the protruding saucepan handle. Other times they just dug in likely looking places. Other times they hunted for the remains of the bonfire, but the tide had covered the part of the beach where they had picnicked and washed all traces of the ashes away. They tried lying on their stomachs, hoping to see the handle rise up on the horizon before them. They walked miles and miles in circles, quarreling.

In the end they gave it up and went swimming, reluctantly deciding that if Naomi could not remember the place they would have to swallow their pride and go and ask Graham if he could. They did not want to do this.

"I told you we'd lose it," said Rachel.

"You didn't."

"Well, I knew we would, anyway."

"Well, why didn't you say so?" demanded Ruth. "We could have put a mark or something. What's the good of saying you knew we'd lose it when it's lost?"

"Naomi will know where it is," said Phoebe hopefully. "She chose the place to dig. Let's go home and get her."

Naomi was still gardening, planting the remains of the lettuces.

"They don't look like lettuces to me," commented Ruth. "I bet they're weeds and it's one of Big Grandma's jokes. Why are you doing it, anyway?"

"Because I want to," Naomi answered. "Look where you're treading! You've squashed that one flat already."

"It's only bent. I just knocked it. Stop digging for a minute, I want to talk to you."

"You wouldn't like it if someone trod on you and then said you were only bent!"

"I wouldn't care. Listen. Do you remember where we buried that stuff yesterday?"

"Of course I do. Anyway, we left that handle sticking up."

"It's not sticking up now," said Ruth sadly. "We've looked everywhere."

"Big Grandma says it's lunchtime," shouted Rachel, running down the garden path to find them. "And that boy Graham's come and Big Grandma asked him to stay and he's telephoned his mum and she says he can and I can't stop Phoebe being awful to him and I thought you said we'd got to be nice because of his books!"

Ruth and Naomi, immediately grasping the seriousness of the situation, hurried to the rescue and found Graham laying the table in the kitchen as if he had lived there all his life. He took no notice of Phoebe, who was pulling her face into a piglike expression, and making grunting sounds. Ruth and Naomi looked at each other and then at Phoebe, and the next thing she knew she was lying on the living room floor, gagged with a tea towel.

"Listen, you horrible brat!" whispered Naomi. "You behave! We want to borrow his books for one thing."

"And find out if he can remember where we were yesterday," added Ruth.

"If you don't stop being so awful," threatened Naomi, "we'll take you away to somewhere and abandon you."

"Like we did before!" reminded Ruth, referring to the time when Phoebe had so badly disgraced them in town that they had tied her by her windbreaker strings to the candy counter in Woolworth's and left her there. In the end she had been brought home by the police, in bad trouble for stealing chocolate fudge and biting a police officer. When asked why she had done these things she had replied that the fudge was all she could reach, and the police officer's hand "got in her mouth." She had been walloped rather hard and sent to bed. Later she had been dragged to the police station and Woolworth's and forced to make humiliating apologies. No one had believed that she had been tied to the candy counter. She had not been tied up when she was found.

"Nod your head if you're going to behave," ordered Ruth.

Phoebe nodded, pulling awful faces, and the tea towel was removed.

"Pigs," she said.

Graham was mashing the potatoes when they returned to the kitchen.

"How does Graham know where everything is?" asked Rachel.

"He often spends a day up here with me," explained Big Grandma. "He helps me in the garden. Put that tea towel aside for washing, Ruth. It won't be fit for anything now. I hope you did a good job with it," she added, looking at Phoebe as she spoke.

In spite of the good job done on Phoebe the lunch was not a great social success. Phoebe sulked, and Big Grandma suddenly remembered why they had gone down to the beach that morning.

"I take it you found my belongings?" she asked them.

"They were just where we left them," said Ruth truthfully.

"We left them there for next time," added Rachel bravely.

"I want them back," said Big Grandma. "They've lost my frying pan, Graham, among other things, and they think I'm a fool. What do you make of that?"

"I don't know," said Graham.

"Well, I do," said Big Grandma, "and I think they had better be careful!"

"YOU SAID YOU could remember," accused Phoebe.

"Well, I can't now," snapped Naomi, staring helplessly around the beach.

That day a battle began in which Big Grandma attacked, demanding her property, and Ruth, Naomi, Rachel, and Phoebe skulked, evaded, lied, and finally starved. Big Grandma chose the weapons, and the weapon she used was hunger.

For three mornings running Big Grandma gave them raw potatoes and bacon for lunch, to take down to the beach and cook.

The first day they ate candy from the shop until they felt sick, smuggled the potatoes into the garden shed, and found, to their great surprise, that they could not bring themselves to throw the bacon away. In the end Ruth took it to bed with her, and later crept downstairs in the dark and sneaked it back into the fridge.

The second day the shopman said he'd been asked not to sell them so much candy, and they got very hungry, although not hungry enough (they discovered) to enjoy eating raw potatoes. That day the bacon went to a black-and-white collie dog, chained to a gate, with a barrel for a kennel.

"It's not wasted if he eats it," said Ruth, unwrapping the package. The dog took the bacon politely in his mouth, and they waited eagerly for him to swallow the evidence, but instead he spat it out, sighed deeply, and appeared to go to sleep.

"Perhaps he'll bury it," said Ruth hopefully.

"Perhaps it's poisoned," said Naomi.

On the third raw bacon day they realized that they would have to ask for outside help, and they hung around the village waiting for Graham. He didn't turn up, and eventually they got so hungry they decided they would have to go to the house where he lived and ask for him. Ruth and Naomi were unable to force Rachel and Phoebe to do this, so they had to go themselves.

"Two young lasses for our Graham," shouted a man into the house when he heard their request. "Tell him to choose his favorite and I'll have the one he doesn't want!" and he winked at them as Graham came out. "Didn't know you were courting, Graham!"

"I'm not," said Graham. "What do they want?"

"You, of course," said the man, slapping him on the back and winking again at Ruth and Naomi. "You give me a shout if they get too much for you," he called over his shoulder as he left them.

It was very difficult to explain to Graham exactly what they wanted him to do. "You never did!" he kept repeating as they told him the story of the buried cooking things. It seemed he could not believe that anyone could be that stupid, and he could not help letting them see how much he admired Big Grandma's resourcefulness. In the end however, he consented to walk down to the beach with them, and ten minutes later was swaggering appallingly as the saucepan, frying pan, bucket, and all its contents reappeared on the face of the earth. Phoebe, who had been very rude indeed about Graham's abilities to help them, was so impressed she smiled at him.

"Would you like to stay to lunch?" asked Ruth, feeling it was the least she could do.

"Had mine," said Graham. "Shouldn't mind another one though," he added as his natural curiosity overcame his fear of poisoning.

"We didn't bring the matches," discovered Rachel.

"I got some," said Graham, feeling more and more like a hero every minute, and by the time they had finished their bacon and potatoes he was so full of pride that he began to grow reckless. They had to flatter him into saying he wouldn't mention anything more about the buried cooking things to Big Grandma, and it was long and difficult work.

"I'll be off now," he said eventually. "Thank you very much."

"Thank *you* very much," replied Rachel, "you saved us from starving!"

"Any time," said Graham modestly, "any time you want something doing."

"Could you lend us some books?" asked Naomi suddenly. "Any old books would do, just something to read?"

"Books?" asked Graham startled. For a few seconds

he could not imagine what they wanted books for; he himself had almost forgotten such dismal school day things existed. "What for?" he asked, and then suddenly remembered listening to Mrs. Sayers's description of her granddaughters. Too many books, he had been told, were one of the chief causes of the girls' inability to behave like rational human beings. Mrs. Sayers, he knew, intended to reform her grandchildren that summer.

"Books to read," explained Naomi as patiently as she could.

"Well," said Graham, unsure of what to do. After all, he didn't want to reform anyone, he wanted to carry on being a hero. There they were, thinking he was marvelous, waiting for him to supply them with books. "Well, I'll have to ask Mum. She's a great one for reading. See you now."

"Very shifty," commented Ruth as he turned his gallant back on them and, once again, almost ran away.

"He didn't want to be roped into carrying this stuff back," said Naomi.

"THREE *Reader's Digest*s!"

"Is that all he brought?" said Naomi, picking weeds out of her row of radishes. "Didn't he bring any proper books?"

"He said his mum got them from the village jumble sale. He said they were all he could find. They're dated nineteen sixty-six. They were left over."

Naomi thumbed through one with a grubby hand.

"All the quizzes are filled in. I hate *Reader's Digest*s. They don't even have a people page."

"And no books coming from home either! Too heavy to send! They've got plenty of money."

"They're spending it all. They'll probably have even less by the time we go back."

"We ought to save these until we're nearly going mad," said Ruth. "At least they're better than cookery books and Shakespeare."

"I am nearly going mad," said Naomi. "Pass me another—this one's useless."

Squatting in the radish row, and hunched on the stony path, Ruth and Naomi read their entire summer's supply of literature in just under an hour. Then they went in for lunch.

IN THE KITCHEN of the farmhouse nearest the sea, Graham's mother asked, "And what do you think of Mrs. Sayers's four? Are they nice lasses?'

Graham shuffled through his brain for a word to describe Ruth, Naomi, Rachel, and Phoebe.

"They're funny," he said firmly.

Chapter 9

<<<<<<<<<<<<<<<<<<<<<<<<<<<

"DEAR EVERYONE," wrote Naomi.

We got your postcards thank you, so this is a nice
letter like you said. They are all saying, Naomi,
write this for me if you are writing to Mum because
they are all too busy (they say). Ruth says it is true
that we cannot have read every one of Big
Grandma's books, but didn't you know no one can
read Shakespeare? We have read all the cookery
books. Ruth says not to worry about Rachel's
clothes because Big Grandma has started taking
them off her when they are terrible. Phoebe wears
clean ones all the time, anybody's, not just hers, so
you don't need to encourage her.

It is quite good on the beach. We've been
swimming a lot and you know how well Ruth can
swim, well yesterday she swam right out so far we
could not see her. We waited quite a long time until
we thought she wasn't coming back and we were
just packing up to go home when we suddenly saw

her. She wasn't tired but she couldn't walk really, and when she could breathe she said: "I swam half way to the Isle of Man. England was on one side and the Isle of Man was on the other and they looked both the same size so it must have been half way." We told Big Grandma who was cross (as usual) (about some bones) and she said: "Why did you come back?" Ruth said next time she wouldn't. But it would be lovely if she could swim all the way only it is too far to swim there and back (she says). If you sent the money she could do it and get a boat back.

We have met a boy called Graham. He says he's never read a book except at school. He's going to teach me to drive a tractor.

It was awful here when it was raining but it's a lot better now. But Big G. is still a slave driver. Rachel and Phoebe are chopping off each other's heads with the firewood ax.

Love, Naomi.

Naomi finished this well-intentioned but extremely alarming letter to her parents and turned to see what her sisters were doing.

"Are we having a nice time?" asked Rachel, looking up from the diary which she had recently begun to keep, the general booklessness of Big Grandma's house having forced her to begin writing one of her own.

"You're supposed to write your own ideas in a diary," Ruth told her, "not everyone else's. I wish you'd let me see it. Why don't you?"

"It's secret."

"It's going to be yours and Naomi's shared Christmas present," explained Phoebe, who had heard. "I'm having a nice time. You can put that in if you like."

All by herself Phoebe had acquired a new hobby. It was her own invention. Nobody had helped her, nobody but Phoebe would even have thought of it. You filled a bucket with water, tied a bit of string on the end of a stick, held the stick over the water, and there you were. Fishing in a bucket. The total hopelessness of the activity was very soothing. It was the perfect sport. Without the emotional stresses of success and failure, she was entirely free to enjoy the pleasures of the moment. She could take liberties that conventional fishermen only dream of. She could stir the water vigorously with her rod and produce no ill effects. She could carry her water to any more convenient site. As a last resort she could chuck it all away, in favor of another bucketful. It was a good hobby, and cheap, and if more people did it more often . . .

Rachel was writing a diary of the summer holiday. At first she had considered the idea of going back to January, when most diaries begin, but she had decided not to bother. Anyway (owing, no doubt, to the fact that she had not kept a diary), she could not remember anything that had happened in January.

"The First Day," she wrote at the top of page one, and carefully underlined it. Her pencil, toothmarked right down to its point, bit into her fingers as she thought backward in time until she reached the cans of dog food she had discovered under the kitchen sink. Were they still there? And what if they weren't? There had been more than one meat pie served in the house since they'd arrived, and Rachel had always eaten her fair share, more if she could get it. What if they had been dog-food pies after all? Shoving her diary under the hedge, Rachel hastened to the kitchen to check.

"What are you doing?" asked Naomi, who had followed Rachel into the house.

"What are you doing yourself?" questioned Rachel, watching as Naomi turned on the faucet and carefully ran hot water over the corner of her mother's envelope.

"Nothing." Naomi peeled off the stamp, positioned it carefully on her own envelope, and hammered it firmly with her fist.

"Looks a bit smudgy," commented Rachel, inspecting the result.

"Mailman won't notice." Naomi moved to the kitchen sink and began measuring out a gallon of water, four milk bottles full, very splashily into a bucket. "What's up with you, anyway?" she questioned, watching Rachel groveling worriedly at her feet.

"I'm looking to see if that dog food's still there," whispered Rachel, glancing apprehensively at the window where Big Grandma, outside, was painting the window frame around the new pane of glass. "What if we've eaten it?"

"I'd rather not know, so you needn't bother telling me."

Fearing the worst, Rachel raked around the bottom of the cupboard until she rediscovered the rusty cans. There were still three of them, so she was safe, and very relieved she scrambled to her feet.

"Well?" asked Naomi, as Rachel headed back to her diary, "go on, say it, we've eaten them, haven't we?"

"You said not to tell you!" remarked Rachel in surprise.

"How many? All of them? You might as well say, now you've made me think of them. Are they all gone?"

"None of them are gone."

"Oh," said Naomi, feeling strangely disappointed, and she began counting drops of Baby Bio into her gallon of water. Five drops to a pint the bottle said, so forty drops to a gallon. Big Grandma watched her through the window.

"What's it for?" she called through the glass.

"My lettuces," replied Naomi. "Their leaves look a bit pale so I thought I'd give them some food." She stirred her bucket carefully with the wooden cake spoon and staggered, lopsided, down the garden path with it. A few moments later she returned for the milk jug.

"There's a little watering can in the greenhouse," Big Grandma told her.

"It's important not to splash the leaves," replied Naomi a bit patronizingly. "A milk jug will be more accurate!"

"Oh," said Big Grandma humbly, and she thought of a whole gallon of Baby Bio being poured on to one short row of lettuces and hoped it would not drown them.

RUTH, HAVING SPENT most of the afternoon trying to teach herself to read upside down from a *Reader's Digest* magazine, now sat on the hillside above an unsuspecting badger's set, waiting for dusk. According to her natural history book, that was the time when the badgers would emerge to tidy up their homes, play with their cubs, and generally provide a pleasant and amusing spectacle.

From her position on the hillside Ruth could see right down into Big Grandma's garden. Naomi was there, hunched like a snail over her lettuces, willing them to grow. The white spot on the path beside her must be her letter. Ruth, who had been allowed to read the letter, rather wished Naomi had minded her own business about the boat money for coming back from the Isle of Man. Certainly her mother would send it; Ruth was sure that swimming to the Isle of Man was just the sort of fresh air, interesting, outdoor pastime that Mrs. Conroy would approve of.

"That will be a nice, healthy way for Ruth to spend the afternoon," she could imagine her mother saying as she pushed the return fare into an envelope, leaving Ruth with no choice in the matter. Half of Ruth wanted to swim to the Isle of Man very much, but the other half did not.

Ruth sighed, and stopped looking at the horrible letter. There was Phoebe, polishing the kitchen window with Big Grandma pointing to the places she had missed. There was Rachel, lurking behind the compost heap, surreptitiously fishing in Phoebe's bucket. Beyond Big Grandma's house was the village, and after that there was just one farmhouse between the village and the sea. Graham's house. Graham no longer thought they were mad, not dangerously mad, anyway, but he still thought they were soft in the head. You could tell.

"Do you know where there are any badger sets around

here?" Ruth had asked him when he came up with the books.

"Badger holes?" asked Graham, grinning. "Haven't you had enough of holes?"

"Oh stop gloating!" said Ruth crossly. "I just wanted to see some badgers, that's all."

"You can always spot a badger hole," went on Graham, undeterred, "by the great heap of saucepans and frying pans lying around outside!

"He keeps them," went on Graham, ignoring Ruth's expression, "to throw at the ghosts and spooks that are always hanging about outside his hole . . .

"Trying to borrow his books!" ended Graham in triumph.

So Ruth had gone hunting for badger sets alone, unguided by anything except her book, which she had decided was not as useful as she had thought it would be in Lincolnshire. It said that badger sets were often occupied by rabbits or foxes, but it did not go on to say how you could tell if you were sitting outside a fox's badger hole, or a rabbit's badger hole, or a badger's badger hole. Ruth had found three burrows, side by side, dug in the hill above the house, and she had examined the bare red earth around them for footprints, but found nothing to indicate whose holes they might be. The only thing to do was to wait and see who came out, and she remembered her book had stressed the importance of sitting downwind of the set, so that the badgers would not smell you.

It's sideways wind now, thought Ruth. It's changed since I came out. And got colder.

The sun slipped behind a thick cloud bank that hung

low over the horizon, and all the colors in the landscape lost their daytime glow. A train came tearing into the village station, and Ruth counted its cars as it passed the signal box. Twenty-eight. The noise of the train rattled and roared through the dusk, echoing off the hillside until it faded away up the coast. Nobody was in the garden anymore. The badgers should be coming out soon and Ruth strained her eyes to stare at the empty patch of ground where she expected them to appear. It was still empty, and the wind through the bracken made distracting rustling sounds, and in the ink-misty village a farm dog barked and barked. Ruth hoped it would not frighten the badgers, who still had not appeared. Perhaps they could smell her. Ought she to have disguised her smell? But then the badgers would have smelled the disguised smell. It was all very difficult.

A soft wooden hooting sounded, over and over again.

Owl, thought Ruth without opening her eyes.

The grass smelled nice.

A noise woke Ruth, and with an awful jump she cracked her head on a rock. There were very loud screamings and mixed-up yells. Big Grandma and Naomi and Rachel and Phoebe were all standing at the bottom of the garden in the dark, bawling her name.

"Coming!" she shouted, slipping and tumbling through the bracken, but the noise continued. Nobody could hear her reply; they were all making such a racket themselves. Among the voices she could hear Graham, but he wasn't calling her name.

"Eh up, come oop, come oop," he was yelling on two flat notes; just the same call as they used to bring in the cows for milking.

"I'm coming!" Ruth shouted again, and this time they heard her and the noises they were making changed to exclamations and mutters and triumphant grunts.

"I fell asleep."

"We know," said Naomi, "we heard you snoring."

"In, in, in," shouted Big Grandma. "The lost lamb has returned. Go in and put the kettle on."

"Lost cow," corrected Graham, meaning no offense. "I called her in with the cows' call. If you were looking for them badgers you had no hope. There's only rabbits in the holes up there."

"You might have said."

"How was I to know?" demanded Graham. "It's lucky I was here to call you down."

"You're always here," Phoebe pointed out.

"So are you," said Graham, "more's the pity!"

"Aren't there badger sets around toward the old quarry?" asked Big Grandma. "Couldn't you take them up there some day, Graham, and show them? Usual rates of course," she added, as if it was a private code.

"I might," said Graham, who was paid fifty cents an hour for doing odd jobs for Big Grandma. "It'll take a bit of time though, it's a fair old walk around there."

"Doesn't matter if it takes all day," said Big Grandma cheerfully. "You can take a picnic and show them the cave."

"Cave?" asked everyone. There were no caves in Lincolnshire.

"When?" asked Naomi.

Graham frowned thoughtfully, as if he were in constant demand all over the village and had to ration his favors.

"Couldn't make it tomorrow."

"Why not?" demanded Rachel.

"The next day then?" suggested Big Grandma.

Graham shook his head as if it wasn't going to be easy.

"Couldn't come Sunday, either," he said. "Mum wouldn't like it. Monday I'll take them, if nothing comes up."

NAOMI'S LETTER arrived in Lincolnshire three days later. The mailman delivered it to her father as he left the house for work in the morning, and he charged Mr. Conroy for the delivery because the letter only had a used stamp. Mr. Conroy did not think much of this, and he stuffed the letter rather crossly in his pocket instead of taking it in to his wife. He did not take it out again until morning break, at which time he forgave Naomi completely. Secretly he had been rather worried to think that his girls were having as bad a time as they had previously described, and when he and his friends had finished laughing at the letter and had all agreed that his daughters must be having the time of their lives, Mr. Conroy borrowed a stamp and an envelope and a piece of paper from the office secretary and dispatched an immediate reply:

Grand letter! Be good! Buy a stamp next time. Enclosing some money. Got to rush. All the best.

Love and kisses.

Dad!

He stuck a ten-pound note in the envelope for pocket money and put it in the mail.

"Ten pounds was far too much!" said Mrs. Conroy when she heard about it later. "You know it will go on nothing but candy," and she settled down to write a long letter to her daughters, all about not playing with axes and not messing about with tractors and not swimming out too far and not spending all that money their father sent on candy and making sure they changed their clothes regularly and not grumbling about being expected to help and how much she was missing them, and that she knew they were far too young to read Shakespeare, and that they were not to try and learn to cook unless their grandma really didn't mind. And that they were never to mail letters without stamping them first.

"OH, DO CHEER UP, Graham, for goodness' sake!" said Big Grandma on Monday morning. "Think of the money!"

"I am," answered Graham, and after making a valiant attempt at smiling he led her granddaughters away.

Naomi carried a knapsack stuffed full of the main part of the picnic, while Ruth had a very awkward shopping bag containing half a gallon of orange squash, her natural history book, and a notebook and pencil. A very shiny red plastic handbag ("I won it at a charity drive," explained Big Grandma) was filled with candles and matches to be used for exploring the cave and carried by Phoebe, who instead of traveling along at her normal half-trot, insisted on playing Old Ladies.

"It's that awful handbag taking her over," observed

Naomi as she watched Phoebe complacently waddle along, hands folded in front of her imaginary bust, and the squashy red handbag swinging gaily from her elbow and bashing her knees.

Big Grandma had also unearthed an old-fashioned leather satchel that she said had belonged to their mother. It was strapped across Rachel's shoulders now, and full of apple tarts.

Graham, as guide to the party, went ahead, carrying nothing at all except a big stick that he had brought with him when he came to collect them. Whenever anyone said, "Graham, swop! You ought to carry something!" he walked a little faster, but when the handles of Ruth's shopping bag snapped under the weight of the orange juice, he did help her to tie up the top with a piece of binder twine and fasten it onto the end of his stick. Then Ruth could carry it very comfortably across her shoulder, like a tramp.

They were following a sheep track which curved around the side of the hill like a narrow belt.

"How far is it?" asked Rachel.

"'Bout three miles or so."

"How far's three miles?"

"From your gran's to the sea is about one mile," answered Graham, "so it's three of them there and three of them back. The badger holes are about halfway along."

"It's the quarry we really want to see," explained Naomi.

"Nothing to see really."

"What about the cave?"

"Cave's a good one," agreed Graham. "I took your gran to it once."

"She'd like a cave," said Naomi. "She'd feel at home there."

They had walked around the curve of the hill, and the village was already out of sight, hidden by the shoulder of the hill. The sheep track had crumbled away in places, and they had to scramble across the narrow shelf that remained, clinging to bracken fronds to help them keep their balance. At other times they found that the path would jump suddenly up and over a boulder or crag that was in the way.

"How do sheep get along," asked Ruth, "with no arms to pull themselves up with?"

"Sheep'll go anywhere if you don't hurry them," Graham said. "It's only when you rush them that they get stuck."

There was a pause at the badger sets.

"Rabbit holes," said Naomi. "Come on, let's get to the cave."

"Badger holes," said Graham. "Seen enough?"

"Where are the badgers, then?" asked Rachel.

Ruth was carefully inspecting the diggings. New red earth, still looking crumbly, as if it had just been dug. Piles of shabby-looking bracken, perhaps left out to air. Beneath the holes was a terraced-shaped mound, made from the soil excavated by generations of hardworking badgers. Ruth hung over a trail of footprints leading through the newly dug earth, drawing a picture of a paw mark in her notebook.

"Coming in a minute," she said without looking up.

"They've all gone," said a voice from the earth, and Ruth saw the top of Phoebe's head sticking out of one of the holes.

"There's nothing in this one," said Phoebe, "I've looked!"

"Get out!" exclaimed Ruth, yanking up her little sister by her arms. "Barging in like that! Serve you right if they bit you! Rude pig! Come on before they explore the cave without us."

"They can't," said Phoebe complacently. "I've got the candles."

The sheep track widened and became a path, and the path curved around to join an overgrown track that led up to the quarry from the main road.

"That's the way the wagons came," Graham told them. "My grandad can remember when it was still used. It's not been worked for years now though. You'd better watch out for vipers here; it's a bad spot for them. Grandad remembers someone getting bitten up here once."

"Did they die?"

"She did. It was a little girl, and her dad was so upset that he waited up here with his shotgun for four days and nights until he got the snake that did it."

"How'd he know he shot the right one?"

"'Course he knew!"

"What about something to eat?" asked Ruth, "and what about the cave? Where is it?"

"Show you after dinner," said Graham, "if there's anything left fit to eat after Naomi's finished sitting on it."

"I'm only leaning on it," said Naomi, wriggling out of the knapsack straps. "It'll still be all right. Look and see."

Graham reached for the bag and began pulling things out. "Package of chocolate cookies. Box of sandwiches. Hang on"—he paused to take one apart—"meatloaf sandwiches."

"I'm not eating that one now," interrupted Phoebe.

"Bag of cracked boiled eggs," went on Graham, ignoring her, "bag of squashed tomatoes—you must have sat on them—pork pie, cut into chunks . . . What's this?" He unfolded a damp brown paper parcel. "Oh, bag of bent bananas."

"Bananas are naturally bent," said Naomi. "Anything else?"

"No," said Graham, feeling around. "Oh, yes, five flat packages of potato chips!"

"We always squash our chips before we eat them," Rachel told him. "It makes them last longer."

Half an hour later the contents of the rucksack, both squashed and solid, had almost disappeared from view.

"I never thought we'd get through that lot," commented Ruth.

"Never should have without Rachel," said Graham. "Don't your jaws ache, Rachel?"

"No," said Rachel vainly, as she sat with the last hard boiled egg in one hand and the last apple tart in the other, taking alternate bites.

"Mine would," said Graham, stuffing rubbish into the knapsack. "We'll go and look at that cave in a minute, if you like."

"I'm too full to move," said Phoebe.

"What did they used to dig here for?" asked Rachel, looking around at the overgrown sides of the quarry.

"Slate," replied Naomi.

"May have been slate," said Graham, settling his head more comfortably on the rucksack full of papers and banana skins. "May have been slate. Or gold or diamonds or pearls." He yawned.

"What's that place down there?" asked Ruth, pointing to another small village visible on the coast beneath them.

"Nothing of a place," said Graham, opening his eyes again. "Proper dump that is."

"It looks just the same as our village."

"It doesn't," said Graham. "They're right queer folk there."

"Why?"

Never stop asking questions, thought Graham. Never a minute's peace!

"Why are they queer folk there?"

"Why are they?"

"Graham?"

"They grow that much barley," mumbled Graham through his dreams, "and they talk that broad."

The girls glanced knowingly at each other and then sat in silence, watching Graham's mouth slowly open wider and wider.

"Not yet," whispered Naomi.

Graham snored.

"Now!"

Very slowly and carefully they got to their feet and

tiptoed away until they were out of danger of disturbing their guide.

"We'll find it ourselves," said Naomi. "I'm sick of being shown the way to everywhere."

"What about snakes?" asked Rachel.

"Fairy stories," replied Naomi. "Same as gold and diamonds and pearls!"

"Snakes always get out of the way, anyway," said Ruth. "It says so in my book."

Slowly they began to make their way toward the quarry face. Elder bushes had grown up since it had been abandoned, and everywhere brambles trailed over the ground like tripwires. Phoebe started picking blackberries and putting them in her handbag.

"Millions of flies," said Ruth. "Oh! Look!"

"What?"

"Just behind that dark tree."

It was hard to believe they had been so close without seeing it. A huge, black, wedge-shaped hole split into the quarry wall straight in front of them. There was a narrow stream pouring out of it, along the side of which ran a gravelly track.

"There's a path," said Rachel.

"We found it without a path," said Ruth.

They gathered at the mouth of the cave and peered inside. It was much bigger than they had expected, and much darker. Near the entrance, ferns and mosses glowed green against the wet walls. The stony path led the way confidently inside and then ended in a black blur. There was a continuous ring and tinkle of drops falling from a height into deep water.

"Oh, no!" said Rachel, backing away.

" 'Oh, no' what?"

"I'm not going in there."

"Well, we are," answered Ruth. 'You can wait here if you like."

"For Graham," added Naomi. "Let's hurry up before he comes. Don't light the candles until we've seen it properly in the dark." Tentatively she began to lead the way inside along the track. Ruth and Phoebe followed her until the darkness grew too much for them to challenge any longer, and all three of them came to a halt. It was a relief to turn around and see the bright triangle of light that was the entrance of the cave and the small dark shape of Rachel, hovering uncertainly in the background.

The candles, slimy and dripping with squashed blackberry juice ("Like lumpy blood," remarked Naomi, wishing to add a little more to the general atmosphere), were extracted from Phoebe's bag.

"Come on, Rachel," called Ruth, and an echo repeated the invitation over and over again.

The candle flames burned straight and clear, their light reflecting off the walls and the pool of water that filled the end of the cave. The sight of them glowing in the darkness enticed Rachel along the path.

"Is it safe?" she asked.

"Safe?" questioned the echo in a very scared voice.

"Do your owl calls," ordered Naomi.

Rachel had one musical accomplishment. She could cup her hands and blow inside them, and produce a deep wooden fluting sound, quite unlike any owl heard in real life, but very impressive.

Squatting in the circle of candlelight, resting her elbows on her knees, Rachel began to blow.

The space around them filled with sound.

"More," whispered Naomi. "Louder!" and Rachel blew and blew on her hands and sent echoes peeling and droning and humming off the shining candle-lit walls. Graham found them crouched around the ring of flames like four witches, all hypnotized by the throbbing reflections of Rachel's melancholy notes.

"Pack it in!" shouted Graham, shocked by the unholiness of the sounds. "You'll call something up, howling away like that! Come on out! You could freeze in here!

"You give me the spooks," said Graham as they joined him in the sunlight. "I close my eyes a minute, and I wake up to that horrible sound and I find you sitting there half daft looking like four clock hens. . . ."

"Speak English," said Naomi.

"Sitting there like one o'clock half struck," continued Graham, "like them old hags in that play we did at school . . ."

"What play?"

"Omlette."

"He means *Macbeth*," Ruth said.

The sun shone cheerfully on their candle-smoked faces and greasy hands.

"What next?" asked Rachel.

"You might like to sneak off somewhere else," suggested Graham bitterly. "I was going to show you something but I don't know if I will now."

"We'll find it ourselves then," replied Phoebe.

"What?" asked Naomi. "Come on, Graham, don't start sulking!"

"Will if I like."

"Please oh please oh please," said Rachel.

"Huh!"

They waited patiently.

"Go on then, show us."

"I'm looking at it."

"What?"

"Upstairs," said Graham. "You missed seeing that, anyway."

Everyone stared in the direction he was facing.

"Can't see anything. Are you still looking at it?"

"No," replied Graham. "I've got my eyes shut now!"

"Be like that then," said Naomi crossly. "See if we care!"

"Who's sulking now?" asked Graham triumphantly. "You just follow me. I'll show you."

He led his suitably humbled party behind the elder tree that screened the cave, and pointed upward. Above the lowest part of the opening, separated by about twelve feet of slaty quarry face, was a second, smaller cave. A steep path, rather like a broken stairway, led diagonally up to it.

"That's upstairs," said Graham, once more the knowledgeable guide. "I never showed that to your gran. I never showed anyone before."

"Why are you showing us then?" asked the honored few.

"I'm softhearted," said Graham. "Are you coming up?"

"After you," said Ruth politely, although Rachel and Phoebe were already scrambling above her.

"I'll go last," said Naomi, who was developing a strange tingling sensation in the soles of her feet.

Ruth and Graham followed Rachel and Phoebe up the path. It was so solid and the steps so evenly placed that despite its narrowness they could walk up it without needing to use their hands.

"I cleaned this up," remarked Graham. "Took out all the loose bits and weeds and made it firm. Shove up a bit," he added to Rachel, who was perched on the top step swinging her legs over the side.

A broad ledge spanned the cave's entrance which, in comparison with the huge cavern beneath them, was very small, not high enough to stand up in properly and only a few yards deep. Only the very back of the cave was in shadow. The afternoon sun shone straight in and filled the cave with light. It was like sitting in a swallow's nest.

"Good, isn't it?" asked Graham proudly. "Better than that old hole downstairs. You can see for miles."

"Does no one ever come to the caves but you?"

"Not that I know of. Except that time I brought your gran. And my brothers used to, but they don't bother anymore."

"What did she want to come for?"

"Why shouldn't she?" asked Graham reasonably.

Rachel, gazing out to sea to where the Isle of Man lounged small and blue against the horizon, remarked, "That's where we're going to swim to."

"Ruth is," corrected Phoebe.

Ruth hoped that Graham would denounce the idea as impossible, and perhaps know of people who had died in the attempt, but he was too full of picnic and sunshine to argue.

"Oh aye?" he said, and added that he could not swim.

Ruth tried to comfort herself with the thought that perhaps swimming trips to the Isle of Man were so common in this part of the world that they had become hardly worth remarking on. If that were the case it would certainly take away from the glory of the achievement. Always supposing she succeeded.

"When're you going to teach Naomi to drive a tractor?" she asked, changing the subject.

Graham sighed. "I asked my dad about that and he said we weren't insured."

"Does it matter?"

"If she came off and got killed or something it would."

"Well, she wouldn't. Anyway, what difference would it make if she did?"

Graham had asked his father more or less the same question and not understood the answer.

"Perhaps we mightn't be able to claim for a new tractor."

"Oh." Ruth hung over the edge to peer down the stairway and see how Naomi had taken this news. She could see her halfway up, standing with her back to them.

"Come on," said Ruth, dangling over the brink like a stringy Rapunzel.

"I can't," said Naomi.

FOR A LONG TIME Graham and Ruth and Rachel and Phoebe sat in the cave saying, "Can't you just turn around and come up?"

"It's dead easy, Naomi."

"Have you hurt yourself?"

"Even Rachel did it!"

"Are you mad about something?"

"What?" asked Naomi, who hadn't heard a word.

"Shall we come down and give you a hand?"

"Don't come near me," said Naomi. "You'll knock me off."

AFTER ABOUT AN HOUR, during which Naomi had not moved a muscle or spoken one rational sentence, they began to get impatient.

"Look here, Naomi, it's getting late!"

"None of us can get down while you're there!"

"Aren't you hungry?"

"Why not let someone come and help you?"

"Don't come near me," said Naomi.

"Well, we can't just stay here!"

Eventually they gave up trying to reason with her. She refused to turn around to move upward, and she dared not go down. An hour and a half ago she had glanced casually behind her, lost her nerve, and not moved since.

"She's cragfast," diagnosed Graham. "I never heard of someone being cragfast before. I'll have to climb around her and get her down from the bottom."

"You can't," pointed out Rachel. "She won't let anyone touch her."

"I'll not touch her."

"You'll fall off," warned Ruth. "Better let me see if I can get around her—I've got longer arms than you."

"I brought you here," said Graham, thinking of his

fifty cents an hour and feeling responsible. "It's not a big drop, anyway."

Swinging himself over the ledge he climbed back down the path to the place where Naomi was stuck.

Naomi screamed in a whisper without moving.

"Be careful!" chorused Ruth, Rachel, and Phoebe, as Graham stood with one foot on the outside edge of the rock, and swung his other leg into space.

"Stand still!" said Graham to Naomi, although standing still was all she had been doing for nearly two hours. A moment later he jumped right past her, landed on the step beneath, pushed himself off with his hands as he hit the quarry side, and half fell, half ran down the steps to the bottom, landing on all fours.

"Glad I cleaned that path up," he said.

"Get your stick," suggested Ruth, but Graham was already running for it. It made a sort of outside banister rail for Naomi, with Graham holding one end two steps in front of her, and Ruth one step behind her holding the other. Then, with Ruth pushing encouragingly in the small of Naomi's back, while Graham steadied her in case she stumbled, they got Naomi down the staircase.

All the way down she made whimpering sounds, and when she reached the bottom she cried. Usually nobody ever saw Naomi cry—if she did it at all she did it alone and nobody knew anything about it. This time, however, she cried in public, very messily because she hadn't got a handkerchief, and she didn't care who saw her.

Not knowing how to deal with a weeping Naomi

made everyone very uncomfortable, and so they ignored her as best they could, running up and down the
staircase to fetch forgotten items from the cave, and
then returning for one last look. Finally, when Naomi's
tears showed signs of turning into mere common-
place sulks, they collected the picnic things and set
off home.

"REALLY, GRAHAM!" exclaimed Big Grandma
when she saw them. "Ten and a half hours you've been
gone, and your mother's been ringing up for you!"

"Call it ten," replied Graham generously. "Oh no, call
it nothing! It's all right, Mrs. Sayers!"

"A bargain's a bargain," said Big Grandma, pushing
something into Graham's hand that Ruth caught a
glimpse of.

"Is that for coming with us?" she asked in surprise.

"What an idea!" answered Big Grandma. "You must
think I've money to waste! Where's Naomi? Have you
left her behind? And where did Rachel and Phoebe rush
off to?"

"They're in the kitchen washing out the handbag, and
Naomi went off down to the shed."

"Problems?" asked Big Grandma.

"Well," said Graham diplomatically, "I'll be off."

"I think," said Big Grandma, as she watched Graham
cycle away down to the village, "I smell a whiff of trouble in the air."

"I smell burning," said Ruth. "It's coming out of the
kitchen!"

"That's your supper," Big Grandma told her. "Burned

shepherd's pie. We'll have to scrape the top off. Go and set the table while I fetch Naomi."

"SHEPHERD'S PIE," said Ruth to Rachel and Phoebe in the kitchen, and Rachel hurried to the cupboard under the sink to count the dog-food cans.

"How many?" asked Phoebe.

"Three. We can eat it."

"What if she bought some new cans and cooked it with them?"

"She'd use the old ones first."

"SUPPERTIME," announced Big Grandma to Naomi, pretending not to notice that Naomi was washing her face in the watering can. "Pull me a couple of lettuces please. And get some tomatoes out of the greenhouse."

"Don't worry!" said Big Grandma, when Naomi only sniffed and turned away. "I'll do it myself. I'm only nearly eighty!"

"You're only seventy!"

"Seventy is a difficult age," said Big Grandma, speaking more to herself than to Naomi. "Your joints get stiff and you've read all the good books and everyone expects you to be a dear old lady."

"No one expects *you* to be a dear old lady."

"Praise be," said Big Grandma. "Have you fought with your sisters?"

"No."

"Graham?"

"No."

"Yourself?"

"I don't know what you mean."

"What happened?"

"I got stuck on the rock and couldn't get down."

"I wish I could dig over that patch where the cabbages were," said Big Grandma, "but I don't suppose I ever will. I believe I mentioned it to you before?"

"Do you want me to do it this minute?" asked Naomi. "In the dark?"

"Tomorrow would do. What else did I miss?"

"Rachel hooted in the cave and scared Graham. Phoebe made Ruth angry by crawling down a badger's hole to look for badgers."

"Tell on, tell on," urged Big Grandma, giving Naomi the tomatoes to carry and leading the way back to the house.

"Graham fell asleep with his mouth open. He snored."

"Burned shepherd's pie for supper," said Big Grandma. "Any more thrilling events? Hope you don't mind it burned?"

"We can scrape the top off," said Naomi. "Ruth found a lot more bones for her collection. Leg bones and another head, but they've still got stuff sticking to them."

"Dear God," said Big Grandma. "Quick, Naomi, I can't run. Don't let her put them into the fridge!"

"W HAT Y O U H A V E to do," explained Ruth, consuming pie and salad at a startling speed, "is simply bury them in a large anthill and the ants eat all the meaty bits off."

"How long does it take?"

"Several months—my book says so. Will you dig them up when they're done and mail them to me, Big Grandma?"

"Certainly not!" said Big Grandma.

Chapter 10

◀◀◀◀◀◀◀◀◀◀◀◀◀◀◀◀◀◀◀◀◀◀◀

IT WAS MORNING. Just. A bare gray light seeped in through the windows, into the rooms where Phoebe and Rachel and Ruth and Big Grandma lay fast asleep, and Naomi stood wide awake and dressed. Outside it was either very misty or drizzling with rain, it was difficult to tell which from indoors.

It's rain! thought Naomi as she got outside and felt it. Damn!

But she went, anyway, and far sooner than she had expected she reached the quarry.

Things dreaded, dentists' appointments for example, always come faster than expected. Naomi's thoughts were swinging between two daydreams. One was of herself, dead, and everyone being stricken with guilt. The other was of herself, alive, and everyone being rescued from sheer rock faces in howling gales by Naomi, heroine, Blue Peter gold medalist. Not that she wanted a Blue Peter gold medal of course, but she would enjoy donating it to the school bazaar. That would make their eyes stick out.

Past the badger sets (no badgers about), and on into the quarry and up the path to the big cave. It was very quiet, and the rocks and slopes still clutched the last dim blurs of night around them. There was no wind, nothing but gray light and misty, soaking rain. Here was Graham's precious staircase. The way he'd gone on about it, thought Naomi, you'd think he'd personally gnawed it out of the rock with his teeth. In a couple of minutes she reached the top and glanced around the upstairs cave. Very boring indeed.

Well, I've been here! thought Naomi, and she stuck the notice she had made, NAOMI WAS HERE, in the middle of the cave and put a stone on the top to keep it from blowing away.

Then she started back.

It's easy, she thought, standing on the place where the awful panic of the day before had struck and looking downward.

"Jump then," suggested the nasty spirit that haunts high places and sheer drops. The ragged bramble-bush tangle of the quarry lurched as Naomi stared at it.

It swayed, she thought. No, I swayed. It's too high. And now she was clutching hard onto the wet rocky side of the path.

"Relax!" she told herself, with her eyes screwed tight shut. "It's easy! You climbed up all right!"

She felt herself slip and opened her eyes in alarm. The world seemed to be heaving and swinging. She couldn't see properly.

Hold on, she thought. Mountain Rescue will find you!

Her hands shifted on the wet slate and a bit broke off.

Then her knees caved in. Then, with a huge feeling of relief, she fell.

It should have been noisy, falling like that, not so dead quiet. There should have been trumpets and shrieks and sirens, and huge explosions, but there was only a crack and a bramble-muffled bump. Then there was Naomi, too scared to move because she had heard the crack and didn't know what had snapped. Nevertheless, through everything else she felt faintly triumphant; she'd known she would fall and she had fallen, so she had been right all along. And she was glad to be down.

Gradually, like a hedgehog unstartling, she began to uncurl.

Not my legs, she thought as she felt them move. Not my back, or I'd be dead. It must be an arm.

Opening her eyes she sat up and felt a dreadful yank on her left side. She looked down, and quickly looked away again.

Her left hand had suddenly betrayed her. She had never put it in that outrageous position in her life. For a minute she thought she might start screaming, but then a golden thought arose and saved her. They'd get a rotten shock when she got back and showed them. She pictured their faces and hoped they'd all faint. She even managed a bit of a grin, a very small one though, and it nearly turned into something else.

With her faithful, untreacherous right hand she picked up her left, put it in her windbreaker pocket, recovered from the shock of the pain, stood up, was sick on her right foot, and walked home.

"HERE SHE IS," announced Phoebe, who had been staring through the kitchen window as Naomi trudged up the garden path.

"She's not still upset about yesterday is she?" asked Ruth.

"She doesn't look as if she is. She just looks . . ."

"Furious," finished Phoebe, as Naomi stamped into the room.

"I've broken my arm," said Naomi.

"Why?" asked Phoebe.

"Look at you!" snapped Big Grandma, before Naomi even had time to get in properly. "You're absolutely soaked! And I wish you children would learn to wipe your feet before you come in! Go and put on some dry clothes!"

"I've broken my arm," said Naomi.

"What for?" asked Phoebe.

"I can't be bothered with arguing," said Big Grandma. "Go and get changed, and be quick about it if you want any breakfast!"

"What do you mean?" asked Ruth.

"I've broken my arm," said Naomi wearily. "Can't you even understand that?"

"Is it still raining?" asked Rachel. "I think I've left my diary outside."

"You haven't really broken your arm, have you?" asked Ruth. "Neither of them look broken to me."

"Well, I have."

"Don't just sit there, Naomi," exclaimed Big Grandma, impatiently joggling the chair into which

Naomi had collapsed. "Go and take your wet things off! You've been told enough times!"

"I've broken my arm," repeated Naomi, as if the phrase were an evil charm. "I heard it crack. Do something."

A WHIRLWIND OF SWEET TEA, phone calls, aspirin, hot water bottles, hysterics (by Rachel), blankets, and conflicting orders swept through the kitchen. Worn out and bad-tempered Naomi sat in the eye of the wind, untouched by the storm that was swirling Big Grandma and her sisters in twisted circles about the house. Then, at the sound of a car door slamming, the wind suddenly stopped, and Naomi and Big Grandma were gone, with nothing left of them but some cut-up pieces of windbreaker lying on the kitchen floor.

"Do you think it hurt?" asked Phoebe.

"Nobody cares if I got hurt," said Rachel, who had been slapped good and hard to stop her screaming.

"Selfish little pig!"

"I don't care. It made me feel sick."

"I thought you wanted to be a nurse," said Ruth. "You'd make a lovely nurse, screaming your head off every time you saw a patient! Nurses see much worse things than that!"

"I like seeing it," remarked Phoebe vainly. "I'd like to watch them cut it open and nail it back together again, too."

"They sew it, not nail it."

"Shut up," said Rachel with her fingers in her ears.

"They sew the skin and stuff," replied Phoebe, "and they nail the bones, and then they plaster it up. I'm going to be a doctor one day. I think it would be lovely."

* * *

NAOMI, on her long walk home, had taken some comfort in the thought that the twenty-mile journey to the hospital would be accomplished in a large, light-flashing, siren-blaring ambulance. Big Grandma, who would also have appreciated the charm of such a journey, understood her disappointment, and sought to make it up to Naomi by driving as excitingly as possible.

"To my mind," she remarked, swerving around a pothole and hooting vigorously at two sparrows squabbling in the gutter, "the National Health Service, *our* National Health Service, lacks, these days, a certain panache!

"They have become," she added, aiming for a cyclist and not missing him by very much, "blasé!" A fly hit the windshield and she put the wipers on double speed to clear it off.

"Give birth to quints," she continued, "receive a brain transplant, contract rabies perhaps, and you might arouse a modicum of interest. Mere human agony however, such as you are now experiencing, they regard as tedious. Not worth the comfort and convenience of an ambulance!"

Glancing sideways she saw that Naomi's face was so white and tight and miserable-looking that she could not speak.

"Poor old thing," said Big Grandma gently.

"NO WONDER they call it a waiting room," commented Naomi, some time later. "They should call it a waiting and waiting and waiting room!"

"Those who do not perish from their injuries," said Big Grandma in a dictating voice, "will certainly die of old age!"

135

At that moment a girl in a white coat, one whom Naomi recognized from the X-ray department and suspected of having sadistically twisted her arm for reasons of private amusement, stuck her head around the door of outpatients and called, "Naomi Conroy?" She caught Naomi's glowering eye and smiled innocently.

"You've broken your arm."

Naomi rolled her eyes to the ceiling and sighed.

"We realized that, dear," said Big Grandma.

"We'll call you in a minute," the nurse added, smiled again, and disappeared.

Big Grandma and Naomi counted the minutes and when it came to forty-two Naomi was taken through to be stretched and pulled into a plaster cast.

"We find quite a lot of children enjoy this part," remarked the doctor untruthfully, for Naomi did not forbear to scream and flinch whenever she felt it needful.

"Why?" asked Naomi.

"Anyway," he said, "you'll be able to get your friends to sign it."

"Why?" asked Naomi.

"Well, that's what people do," replied the doctor, still with his awful fake cheerfulness.

BIG GRANDMA had spent a dismal morning, restraining Naomi, helping her count the red, green, and white tiles on the floor and calculating the percentage covered by each, and reading and solving all the problems on the problem pages in the magazines. Left alone she had mentally redesigned the waiting room (money no object). She had added hammocks and a bar and was just choosing the drinks when Naomi, equipped with plaster and painkillers, reentered the room.

"All things come to those who wait," she remarked, heading immediately for the door.

"I tried to hurry," said Naomi, pathetically but loudly, "but I had to stay while the doctor made a lot of jokes about people with broken bones."

There was a murmuring sound of anger from all the people in the waiting room who had, or suspected they had, broken bones.

"Poor little girl," remarked the white-coated nurse to the doctor as he left to call up the next of their victims.

"Poor little girl my . . . foot!" said the doctor.

"WHAT ARE YOU DOING?" Rachel asked Ruth as she met her staggering in from the garden with an armful of roses and daisies.

"Getting ready for Naomi. Come and help."

Together they proceeded to ransack the house, systematically going through every room in turn and removing anything that might be useful.

"What about Big Grandma's?" asked Rachel. "She hates us going in there. I've only been once and she chucked me out."

Ruth, however, had no such qualms and marched boldly in, seizing a bowl of potpourri from the bedside table en route.

"Anyway, there's nothing in here that Naomi would want," continued Rachel, following Ruth, "no books and nothing to eat. . . . What's that door?"

Ruth, who had been eyeing the bedside rug in a

speculative way, looked up at the question. "What door?"

"This one." Rachel pulled aside a green velvet curtain that was almost hidden behind the shadow of the wardrobe.

"That's a window." Ruth bent down to pick up the rug and dropped the bowl of potpourri, scattering flower petals all over the floor.

"No, it's a door, but it's locked." Rachel tugged at the handle. "It must lead out into nothing though. Into the air. Unless Big Grandma's got a ladder for getting out at night."

Ruth, abandoning the flower petals, came to investigate the door. Then she peered out of the corner window on the other side of the wardrobe.

"It must go into the garage," she announced. "She must have had an upstairs room built on top of the garage when she got the garage made. And that door is where a window used to be. I wonder what she keeps in there?"

"It's too dark to see anything," said Rachel with her eye to the keyhole.

"Well, we haven't time now, anyhow," said Ruth. "Come and help me get this stuff up off the floor. They'll be back soon—it's nearly night already. What's Phoebe doing?"

Phoebe was writing a letter home which simply stated: *We hav run ot of muny.*

She was doing the kisses when the car pulled up and Naomi, half doped with painkillers, staggered out of the back. Sisterly inquiries filled the air.

"What bone did you break? Did you see the X ray? Would you recognize one like it only coming off a sheep?"

"Did you have a nice time? What did you have for dinner? Did you get that plaster cast free for nothing?"

"Did they nail it? Did they nail it?"

"I'm going to bed," said Naomi, pulling a bundle of screwed-up magazines from under her jacket and handing them to Ruth. "Pinched them," she explained, climbing wearily up the stairs. "Tell Phoebe to shut up."

"Shut up," said everyone to Phoebe.

"I've got everything ready," said Ruth proudly, leading the procession to the bedroom.

"Very nice too," commented Big Grandma when she saw the invalid chamber that had been prepared during their absence. Two beer glasses, one full of orange juice, the other full of flowers, stood beside Naomi's bed. Ranged on the floor within easy reach was all the reading matter they possessed, including Shakespeare and Phoebe's coloring book, a plate of cheese sandwiches, a half-eaten bar of chocolate (Rachel's idea), and a rather too obvious bucket.

"You could have made my bed," said Naomi ungratefully.

"Sharper than a serpent's tooth," commented Big Grandma. "And what's my rug doing in here, may I ask? I suppose you've been rifling my bedroom. I've told you to keep out of there. Is nothing sacred?"

"Why've you locked the door that goes into the top of the garage?" asked Rachel.

"To keep you out," said Big Grandma. "Why else?

Anyway, I suppose I'd better have Ruth's bed tonight, and she can have the rack and a sleeping bag in Rachel and Phoebe's room."

"What's the rack?" asked Ruth suspiciously, but it turned out to be only Big Grandma's way of describing a camp bed.

DEEP IN THE NIGHT Naomi lay staring into the dark, listening to the windy sound of Big Grandma's breathing. Her arm hurt very badly. The tablets must have worn off. Her left hand was throbbing.

They've put the plaster on too tight, she thought, and remembered a girl at school who had kept an elastic band around one finger until it went cold and black.

"Gangrene," said Naomi out loud.

Big Grandma gave a sudden snort and woke herself up.

"Are you all right?"

"I was just wondering if I had gangrene."

"No," said Big Grandma firmly, "you haven't."

"I have rotten luck."

"You surely can't want gangrene."

"I meant falling off."

"That was just vertigo. Fear of heights. Nothing to do with luck. Nelson had it, too."

"I thought he had seasickness."

"And vertigo," said Big Grandma. "The poor man had both. Think yourself lucky. Go to sleep."

Naomi lay silent for a while, listening to the nighttime sounds of the house; slow creaks and unknown rustling sounds and the rattle of the branches of the elm tree outside the house.

"Why did Uncle Robert run away?"

"I don't know. It was all a long time ago. Go to sleep."

"Don't you think about him?"

"Not very much," said Big Grandma, truthfully but rather unmaternally.

Naomi ate one of her cheese sandwiches. It tasted horrible.

"D'you mind if I put the light on and read?"

"Very much indeed," said Big Grandma. "Try counting sheep jumping over a gate."

"I don't know what sheep look like jumping over a gate. I didn't know they could jump."

"Try it."

Naomi tried it for a few minutes. "They keep bashing their knees," she said eventually. "Big Grandma?"

Big Grandma dragged herself awake again.

"D'you think this house is haunted? Ruth does."

Big Grandma made an enormous concession, recognizing that if Naomi did not have something to take her mind off her broken arm she was quite liable to lie awake and talk all night.

"I suppose it might be a little bit haunted!"

"Is it?"

"Perhaps a bit," repeated Big Grandma grudgingly. "In a manner of speaking. A rather flamboyant manner of speaking, and not strictly true."

"What by?"

Big Grandma's imagination failed her. "All sorts of things. Go to sleep."

Naomi, suddenly overwhelmed by exhaustion, lay quietly conjuring up ghosts to haunt Big Grandma's house. Strangely enough, all the dim white spirits of her imagination turned, on closer inspection, into sheep. Sheep that ate dog food. Sheep with aching knees and legs in plaster cast. She fell asleep.

Chapter 11

4444444444444444444444444

THE MORNING mail brought Mr. Conroy's letter from Lincolnshire. The ten pound note fell out as soon as they ripped open the envelope.

"They've started sending my money," said Phoebe, very pleased. "At last!"

Rachel, who had been sitting on the end of Naomi's bed chewing up the last of the cheese sandwiches, made a hasty grab for the ten pound note. It ripped in half.

"Mind my cast," said Naomi from the pillows, where Big Grandma had ordered that she should spend the morning. "Anyway, it's Ruth's swimming-to-the-Isle-of-Man money."

Ruth came in at that moment. "Big Grandma says you're not to get up until she says so."

"What, not even to go to the toilet?" asked Rachel and Phoebe in chorus.

"What, not even to go to the toilet?" called Ruth over the banisters.

"Yes, of course to go to the toilet!" shouted up Big Grandma, grinding her teeth.

"But you can to go to the toilet," added Ruth, reappearing in the bedroom.

"I already have," said Naomi. "Look! Dad's sent your Isle-of-Man money already!"

"I don't believe you," said Ruth, not very hopefully.

As proof, Rachel and Phoebe, unprotestingly, each handed her half of a ten pound note. They were very pleased to think she was going to swim all that way.

"Oh," said Ruth sadly. "Oh, well, I might as well do it this afternoon, then. Might as well get it over with."

"Don't forget to send us postcards before you get the boat back."

"I shan't be able to go buying postcards in a swimsuit," protested Ruth.

"Wear your shorts and a T-shirt to swim over," said Naomi resourcefully, "and they'll dry off in the sun as you look for the post office."

"Oh, all right."

"Make sure you eat a lot of lunch. To give you strength."

"What'll you tell Big Grandma when she asks where I am?"

"We'll just say you've gone for a swim," said Naomi. She seemed to have thought of everything.

MRS. CONROY, lying in the faraway Lincolnshire garden having an after-lunch five minutes rest, reread Naomi's latest letter. John was right, she thought; they certainly did sound happier. They should get his letter today, and her own, forbidding the list of enterprises that Naomi had described, tomorrow. Tomorrow. Panic seized her and she rushed into the house and dialed Big Grandma's number.

"Answer, answer, answer," she prayed, having awful visions of Ruth in the middle of the Irish Sea, equipped with her father's ten pound note for the boat home.

"Where's Ruth, Mother?" she shouted frantically when Big Grandma finally answered the phone.

"Whatever's the matter?" asked Big Grandma. "Ruth? I don't quite know at this moment. She said this morning she was going swimming. . . ."

"Oh God, oh God," said Mrs. Conroy.

"But I think she might still be up in Naomi's room," continued Big Grandma, wondering if her daughter had gone mad and if so whether she ought to mention Naomi's broken arm.

"Tell her," shouted Mrs. Conroy, "not to swim to the Isle of Man! *Not* to! Go and tell her now!"

"I can't think what you're talking about!"

"Just tell her! Go now. Please go now!"

Better not to mention Naomi's arm, thought Big Grandma. Better perhaps to humor her.

"I'm sure she has no thought of doing such a thing," Big Grandma said as soothingly as she knew how. "But I'll go up and tell her and then I'll get her to call you back."

SHE FOUND Ruth busily engaged in sewing a ten pound note inside a plastic bag to the inside of her shorts. Naomi was studying a map in the back of a guidebook that had been purchased only that morning. Rachel and Phoebe sat on the window seat gazing out toward the horizon with their mouths already hanging open in admiration.

"Looks about forty miles," she heard Naomi say cheerfully. "But the tide's going out. That'll help a lot."

"Yes," agreed Ruth dolefully.

"You've already swum halfway without even trying."

"Yes."

"You are lucky. I wish I was going. Just my luck to break my arm."

Ruth thought she would much rather have a broken arm but did not say so.

"But, anyway," said Naomi generously, "you can swim much better than me. I don't really think I could do it even if it wasn't broken."

Ruth thought that even with two perfect unbroken arms she was going to find the journey extremely unpleasant, but obviously it was far too late to protest.

"Could it be," asked Big Grandma, who had been listening behind the door hardly able to believe her ears, "that Ruth is planning a little trip?"

"To the Isle of Man," said Rachel. "Dad sent the boat money to get back."

"Forty odd miles?" said Big Grandma.

"That's what we worked it out to be," agreed Naomi.

"By strange coincidence," said Big Grandma, "your mother has just this minute telephoned. Cancel all plans, Ruth. She says you can't do it!"

"Can't do it?" asked Ruth, looking up for the first time.

"Absolutely forbidden," said Big Grandma, "and you're to call her up at once and tell her you know."

"Oh damn," said Ruth, her face shining with relief. "I was just getting ready to go!"

"Go and speak to your mother."

Ruth, hardly able to believe her good fortune, hurried downstairs. She returned a few minutes later.

"She says you're not to learn to drive a tractor," she said to Naomi.

"Can't, anyway, with a broken arm," said Naomi.

"Quite," said Big Grandma. "Did you tell her about Naomi's arm?"

"I thought Naomi would rather tell her herself," said Ruth virtuously.

A QUIET TIME followed Naomi's accident. It was ordered by Big Grandma, who threatened to send them home to their parents if she did not have a little peace and tranquillity in which to marshal her forces. It was surprising that instead of seizing joyfully on this promise of escape, the girls made an honest attempt to become less troublesome guests. Although they still disapproved of very many aspects of their enforced holiday, they no longer wanted to escape. Big Grandma had thought she might have to buy her peace with literature, despite all her resolutions, but this turned out not to be the case. Her granddaughters used the time to develop their own peculiar interests.

Rachel's diary, the future Christmas present of her sisters Ruth and Naomi (and perhaps Phoebe, too), was finally brought up to date. A certain amount of one-armed gardening was done, too, and a great deal of fishing in buckets. Badger-baffling disguises were attempted and discarded.

"I am afraid you will only succeed in repelling them even further," remarked Big Grandma when she discovered Ruth's jeans and sweater buried in the compost heap.

"But it says in my book that badgers are frightened and suspicious of human smells," explained Ruth. "Wearing these will stop me smelling so human."

"But no less frightening and suspicious," pointed out Big Grandma, an aspect that Ruth had not considered.

If Ruth's efforts to delude the local wildlife were a failure, Rachel's diary seemed an undoubted success. In it every meal she had eaten that summer had been carefully and accurately recorded. Writing accounts of mere events, she had soon decided, was a waste of time and not at all necessary. For example, she could look at the previous Sunday's entry: "Ordinary breakfast, roast chicken, peas, pots, runny trifle pudding, egg sandwiches, chocolate cake, ginger cookies," and the whole day's happenings would immediately spring to mind and insert themselves neatly between the appropriate meals. Rachel thought that everyone's brain worked this way.

Ruth and Naomi, stationed at the end of the garden so they could watch Naomi's radishes growing while they consulted, spent an afternoon reviewing the supernatural situation.

"And I said, 'How can I go to sleep in a haunted house?' and she said, 'Haunted my foot, and anyway, what do you think I've been doing for thirty-seven years?' "

"Wasn't she even scared?"

"Just bad-tempered because I'd woken her up again."

"Perhaps that's why Uncle Robert ran away—because the house had a ghost in it."

"More than one I think. Anyway, she doesn't care. It's all right for her; she's old enough to be a ghost herself."

"There's ways of getting rid of them," said Ruth. "You can exercise them or something."

"They probably get enough exercise, tearing around the house all night."

"And I've heard you can keep them out by painting the window frames and the doors bright red. They don't like red. It upsets them."

"It would upset Big Grandma too. She'd go mad."

"Or you can eat garlic."

"I didn't know ghosts could smell things. How do they sniff?"

Graham heard Naomi's last remark as he came sneaking up on them and obligingly sniffed a ghostly and horrible sniff. He smirked with satisfaction as they clutched each other in fright and glared at him.

"Don't look at me like that," he said. "I'm just here for a minute with a message from my mum, and then I've got to go shopping for school clothes. She said to tell you you're all to come to tea tomorrow afternoon."

"Big Grandma too?"

"I don't think so," Graham answered. "I think it's more to give her an afternoon off. Anyway, it's you lot they want to have a look at."

"Who?"

"My brothers. When I told them about you, they said they'd like to have a look," said Graham, "and my mum said to tell you to come to tea and give poor old Mrs. Sayers an afternoon off."

"Thanks a lot," said Ruth at the end of this charmless explanation. "Any more kind remarks or are you going?"

"I'm going," said Graham cheerfully. "See you tomorrow, then. Don't come too early though."

"Why not?" asked Naomi incautiously.

Graham opened his mouth to explain that his father did not want a pack of girls hanging about the farm half the afternoon, but at that moment he caught sight of Phoebe sitting in solitary state beneath the damson tree, earnestly fishing.

"I never seen anything like that," he murmured in amazement, and left very quietly.

MUCH TO EVERYONE'S SURPRISE, Big Grandma took her granddaughters' launch into society remarkably seriously. They must look decent for once, she said; they were not going to afternoon tea with her friends looking (as they so often did) as if they had just been pulled out from under their beds. She made them put on their best (and only) dresses, brought in case Big Grandma ever wanted to take them anywhere special, but she never had.

Ruth's and Naomi's dresses were navy blue, which was Mrs. Conroy's favorite color because it did not show the dirt. The dresses had been made the summer before with good big hems so that she could let them down when they got too short. Her daughters never got any fatter, only taller.

Rachel's dress, newly mended by Big Grandma, was pale pink. It had once been Ruth's flower girl's dress in a wedding, with puffed sleeves, a lace collar, and a pink bow. But, following Graham's invitation, Rachel had secretly altered it with rather blunt scissors. It looked a lot plainer now.

Phoebe, who quite often had new clothes, because Rachel ruined so many of hers before they could be passed on, was in a color her mother described as "pretty emerald" (again, good for not showing the dirt). Her sisters described it as "Marks-and-Spencer's-awful-green" (after the store it had been bought at) and disliked it very much. Phoebe did not look right; her dress, which Mrs. Conroy had wisely remarked, "Would fit when she grew into it," had not yet acquired that desirable state.

When they were ready, Big Grandma held a gloomy inspection. Something looked unnatural, but she could not think exactly what.

"Clean socks!" she ordered, wondering if it would help.

"None left," replied Ruth.

"Well, no socks at all then," said Big Grandma. "And for goodness' sake wash your feet."

"We're going to the beach first," said Naomi. "We'll get them clean there."

"No bathing, then," said Big Grandma, "and keep tidy, and don't get that plaster cast wet, Naomi. And behave yourselves."

"We always do."

"And have a nice time," said Big Grandma.

"WHAT'S THAT?" asked Rachel, as they stopped on the way down to the sea and Ruth extracted a bulging shopping bag from under a hedge.

"Swimming things."

"She said 'No swimming.' "

"She said 'No bathing.' "

"It's the same thing."

"It's not. Bathing's with soap and swimming's just swimming. Anyway, you don't have to."

I'll say they made me, thought Rachel comfortably to herself.

I'll pretend I didn't understand, thought Phoebe.

However, when they reached the beach even Rachel and Phoebe were slightly shocked to see Naomi struggling, one armed, into her swimsuit.

"She said not to get your plaster cast wet," pointed out Rachel.

Ruth and Naomi ignored her. They were doing something with plastic bags and elastic bands.

"Hope it works," said Naomi.

"Plastic's waterproof," Ruth answered, "and they haven't got any holes in, I've checked. Anyway, what would happen if it did get wet?"

"Nothing," said Naomi, thinking hard. "I'm sure I've seen people with broken legs out in the rain."

"She said 'Behave yourselves,' " said Rachel when she realized what her sisters were doing.

"She said 'Wash your feet,' " said Naomi. "So shut up and go and wash 'em."

"And she said 'Have a nice time,' " added Ruth. "So shut up and go and have it."

Mrs. Brocklebank, Graham's mother, stood gazing at her dining room table with pride. There were sandwiches and cakes and roasted chicken legs and bowls of fruit and tomatoes. There was a big apple tart, cut up into slices, and a trifle pudding and a lemon cake with whipped cream on top. There was nothing that could not be eaten one handed.

"Won't be enough there," said Graham, coming in. "That Rachel could eat all of that by herself."

"You do talk some rubbish," said his mother, laughing. "They none of them look as if they'd ever had a square meal in their lives!"

"You wait and see," Graham told her. "Great platefuls they eat, and it doesn't have to be anything special either. I've seen them eat raw potatoes and burned bacon like it was Sunday dinner!"

"They must be half starved," said Mrs. Brocklebank.

Graham's grandad, who always came to tea on special occasions, was sitting listening. Sometimes he wouldn't speak all day, but then he always made up for his silence on other days, by shouting. He always shouted, he was deaf, except when it suited him to hear. Now he shouted, "They must 'ave worrums!"

"Do be quiet, Dad," said Mrs. Brocklebank. "You shouldn't talk like that. It's not nice!"

"Mittering and muttering," shouted Graham's grandad. "I can't 'ear you!" and he fell silent again, staring at the table. Some days he could be very awkward.

"IT'S GONE SOGGY at the top," said Naomi.

"It'll dry."

"I'm stuck." Naomi writhed inside her half-on dress, trying to force her plastered arm through the sleeve.

"You should have dried before you got dressed," Ruth

said as she stuffed her sister into her clothes. "Now you're covered in white stuff."

"So're you!"

Navy blue, while an excellent color for not showing dirt, was a dismal failure when it came to concealing damp plaster-of-paris smears. Scrubbing at the marks with a wet handkerchief dipped in seawater only made them worse.

"You'll get into trouble," Rachel remarked.

"Stop standing on Phoebe's dress," Ruth ordered, "and put your own on. Where is it?"

Rachel didn't answer.

Phoebe was rubbing sand from between her toes. "It blew away," she said.

"It what?" said Naomi, Ruth, and Rachel together.

"It blew away," repeated Phoebe to her sisters.

"Where to?"

"I don't know. I didn't watch."

"You can't watch something blowing away and not watch where it goes to."

"I can."

It was difficult to spot a pale pink dress on a pale gold beach on a windy, sun-glary day. They spent some time looking until Rachel solved the problem by grabbing Phoebe's dress and squeezing into it. Faced with the prospect of arriving at an unknown house for afternoon tea in only her underpants and sandals, Phoebe suddenly remembered in which direction the dress had blown, and after a short search they fished it up out of a rock pool.

"Do I look all right?" asked Rachel, when they had wrung it out and put it on her.

"Oh, well," said Ruth, looking at her doubtfully.

"Oh, well, what?"

"I wish we'd brought a comb," said Naomi.

MRS. BROCKLEBANK was not a vain woman. Because she had invited people to afternoon tea, she did not expect them to dress up for the occasion. For herself, she didn't bother much about fashion; she believed in being neat and comfortable. It took a good deal to shock her, but Ruth, Naomi, Rachel, and Phoebe, all looking neither neat nor comfortable, managed to do it by walking up her drive.

And their hair's all wet! she thought as she opened the door, and their dresses . . .

"Come along in," she said very kindly. "Come along in. Tea's ready—you're just in time. Do you want to wash your hands or anything?" Not that it would help much, she reflected, when what they really needed was a good bath.

"No thanks," said Phoebe cheerfully. "We've just come out of the sea!"

"And you look like it," remarked Mark, one of Graham's older brothers, who had followed them in.

On the way to the farm Ruth had been chosen to speak for the family, since she was the oldest, and (marginally) the cleanest, so she began,

"I'm sorry . . ."

"We're in the dining room," said Mrs. Brocklebank. "You come in and make yourselves at home. And you go and clean your boots up," she added to Mark, "trailing in muck and acting so cheeky. This is our Peter," she continued, shepherding them along in front of her and nodding to the person who had teased Rachel and Naomi earlier in the summer when they had come for help in digging up a frying pan, "and that's Graham's grandad over by the fire. No need to get up, Dad! Now you know us all. Mr. Brocklebank's away today."

"'E 'ates cump'ny!" shouted Graham's grandad from the fireplace. "Not like me! I like a joke and a laugh I do!" Then he seemed to change his mind and turned so that only his back was visible to the visitors.

In a few moments they were seated around the table. Ruth began again:

"I'm sorry . . ."

"What a lovely supper," said Rachel, eyeing the table with such undisguised greed that Graham could not resist winking at his mother.

"I'm sorry we look a bit untidy," Ruth said desperately (she didn't want anyone to think they didn't know what they looked like), "but we went swimming and Naomi's plaster cast got wet—we put plastic bags on it but it still did—and Rachel stood on Phoebe's dress and the sand was wet, and then it got a bit ripped when she put it on when her own dress blew away, and they had a bit of a quarrel, well, a fight actually, and Naomi had to stop them with her plaster cast."

This honest recital was a great success. The party cheered up tremendously. Peter choked on his chicken leg, and Graham wore the conceited expression of a conjurer who has just produced his first rabbit. Only Graham's grandad was quiet, staring into the fire and drinking tea out of an old cracked mug, the only one he would ever use. He carried it around in his pocket.

The girls talked and talked. It was the first time in their lives that they had ever tried to be pleasant, on purpose. Graham was proud of them. And they ate nearly as much as he had prophesied they would. Mrs. Brocklebank, in the pleasure of watching them enjoy her cooking, forgot that she had ever thought of sitting them on newspapers to save her chairs.

Rachel had just neatly turned the conversation to a discussion of Big Grandma's motives in keeping dog food, when Graham's grandad swung around in his chair and roared, "Greedy young beggars!"

In the silence that followed he said loudly, "There's been many a corpse washed up on that beach!"

Graham and his brothers made moaning sounds.

"If you're going to start that, Dad," said Mrs. Brocklebank, who knew too well what was coming. "Why you can't be pleasant I don't know. . . ."

"Have you ever found one?" asked Naomi with a note of envy in her voice.

"I wish we could find one," asked Ruth sincerely, and Phoebe nodded her head in enthusiastic agreement.

"Don't encourage him," whispered Peter, but it was too late.

"Many a one," shouted Graham's grandad, "but mine were worse. It were bad, it were. . . ."

"Enough's enough," said Mrs. Brocklebank. "Pass that cake to the girls, Graham, don't just sit there eating it all yourself."

"It were rotten!"

"What did you do?" asked Naomi, fascinated.

"Me and Jim (you wouldn't know Jim), we see it from the fields, and I says 'twas a corpse, and Jim says 'twere a drowned sheep. By gum, 'e soon knew better. . . ."

"Be back at school before you know where you are," remarked Mrs. Brocklebank. "I don't know where the summer goes to!"

"'E were soon a lot wiser!"

"I don't think we want to hear any more, thank you, Dad!"

"Old Jim runs off for the police. (There was money if you found a body in them days. Bounty. Nowt now, nothing in it.) Well, he runs off for the police and I stay and watch it don't float out again."

"It's his favorite story," Graham explained, "but he usually only tells it when he's drunk!"

"Graham!"

"Know what the police did when he sees it? First thing he done? 'E was sick! Sick! Laugh! Me and Jim did laugh!"

Graham's grandad slapped his leg and roared, and his mug fell off the arm of his chair. Rachel picked it up for him and stood it carefully on his lap.

"Get a cloth one of you boys," said Mrs. Brocklebank crossly, "and you behave yourself, Dad. It was nothing to laugh at, anyway."

Ruth saw that for some reason Mrs. Brocklebank really did not want the story to continue, so she said very cheerfully, "If you wrote down the recipe for that cake, perhaps my mum might make it. If it's fairly easy she might."

"You come around one morning and we'll have a baking day," said Mrs. Brocklebank, "and then when you go back you can make her one yourself."

"Can I come, too?" asked Naomi, relieved to see Mrs. Brocklebank smiling again.

"They got a bit a wood," shouted Graham's grandad, "and they took an arm each and I took 'old of the legs to lift it on like."

"I would have liked a daughter," continued Mrs. Brocklebank valiantly, "and Graham always used to say he wanted a sister."

"To knock about," put in Peter.

"I were smoking Black Twist in my pipe, so it were all right for me, see?"

"Why?" asked Rachel.

"Black Twist were right strong," explained Graham's grandad, "and it like covered the smell. But smell weren't nothing then to what it was when he tried to lift it. . . ."

"If he's upsetting you," said Mrs. Brocklebank to the girls, "the lads can take him out, and welcome."

"They're enjoying it," said Mark. "Look at their faces!"

"Well, Jim took 'is arm and we all said 'Right then!' and lift together and poor old Jim slips on a rock and fall, and the smell . . ."

"More trifle anyone?"

"Yes, please," said Rachel.

"Like nothing you'll ever have smelled! Like . . ."

"Mark and Peter," ordered Mrs. Brocklebank, "take him out. I've had enough."

"And it look . . ." bawled Graham's grandad as they escorted him to the door, ". . . it look like . . ." They heard the kitchen door slam behind him.

"That there trifle!" came muffled down the passage, and they could hear him groaning with laughter.

"IT WAS A LOVELY supper," said Ruth, when they left for home. "Thank you very much."

"Brilliant," agreed Naomi, "and we really liked listening to Graham's grandad."

"Thank you for having me," said Rachel politely. "I'll put it all in my diary."

"When can we come back?" asked Phoebe.

"You come when you feel like a bit of baking," said Mrs. Brocklebank, "and we'll have a good-bye supper before you go."

"A good-riddance supper," remarked Graham.

"We're not going yet!" said Ruth and Naomi, looking so alarmed that Mrs. Brocklebank hastened to agree that they must have at least a week or two left. "And it's nice to know you're enjoying yourselves so much," she added.

"It's almost perfect," said Ruth, pulling herself together from the shock of hearing eternity described as a week or two, "except that there's nothing to read at Big Grandma's."

"Nothing to read!" exclaimed Mrs. Brocklebank. "Surely she's found you more than enough to keep you quiet all summer!"

"Shakespeare and cookery books," said Naomi, "don't count."

Mrs. Brocklebank was about to reply when she caught sight of Graham standing behind his guests, rolling his eyes, tapping his head, and making corkscrew motions with his finger in the air. Clouting him and telling the girls he'd be just like his grandfather (if not worse) in seventy years' time took her mind off the subject of literature for that time.

"She's not letting them have any books," Graham explained to his mother when she had got him indoors and the girls had gone, "because too much reading sends people barmy. She's curing them."

"What rubbish are you talking now?" asked Mrs. Brocklebank. "Too much reading sends people barmy! I've never heard such nonsense!"

Graham, thinking that his mother had had the evidence before her eyes all afternoon, nevertheless did not bother to argue.

"Did you like them, then?" he asked instead.

"I thought they were smashing lasses."

"But didn't they look awful?"

"They had lovely manners," said Mrs. Brocklebank, stunning Graham into complete silence.

"I DIDN'T KNOW we'd been here so long," Naomi remarked as they trudged back up the hill to Big Grandma's.

"Is it soon time to go home?" asked Phoebe. "Why? I'm not going. Or I'll go home and get my money and come back. With some books."

"We haven't done hardly anything yet," said Ruth. "I wish now I'd swum to the Isle of Man. And I still haven't seen any badgers."

"What was Mrs. Brocklebank going to say about Shakespeare and cookery before she walloped Graham?" wondered Naomi.

"We haven't eaten the dog food yet," said Rachel.

"We haven't found out what's through the door in Big Grandma's bedroom. . . ."

"What door?" interrupted Naomi.

"One we found when you were at the hospital. It goes into the top of the garage. We forgot to tell you about it."

"We can't go home," continued Rachel. "It's school when we go back!"

This appalling reminder caused deep gloom among her sisters. Earnestly each one began to pray the holiday and weekend prayer of the Conroy girls.

"Please God let the school burn down. But let the hamsters and gerbils be rescued. (And the stick insects.) Amen."

Rachel broke the silence first.

"When I grow up," she announced as they neared Big Grandma's, "I bags Graham to marry. I've bagged him now so don't forget. And," continued Rachel, ignoring her sisters' rude remarks, "I will have the farm and all the animals and Graham's grandad and Mrs. Brockle-bank will live with us and do the cooking.

"And for breakfast every day," said Rachel, cheering up tremendously at the thought, "for breakfast every day"—Rachel, whose aspirations to matrimony were of a gastronomic rather than romantic nature, rubbed her stomach in anticipation—"I will have mushrooms, sausages, bacon, tomatoes, eggs, pancakes, honey, and trifle pudding, and for lunch. . . ."

Chapter 12

‹‹‹‹‹‹‹‹‹‹‹‹‹‹‹‹‹‹‹‹‹‹‹‹‹‹‹‹‹‹

THE SUMMER WAS PASSING. It was almost half over. During the weeks in Cumbria the girls had lost track of time. In the beginning it had seemed as if they were destined to an endless exile, the objects of Big Grandma's contemptuous mercy. No one had been able to stop thinking of all the money that was being wasted at home. Then, gradually, the view from the house became familiar. Big Grandma's cooking stopped tasting like an outsider's cooking and became ordinary. Strangers stopped peering at them to see who bore the most resemblance to their much-pitied grandmother. Graham had stopped watching them for signs of madness.

"Mother," said Mrs. Conroy on the telephone to Big Grandma one day, "what on earth are the girls talking about when they say they have no books to read?"

"They haven't," said Big Grandma. "Simple as that."

"Good gracious!"

"I told you they read far too much. Pure escapism. Just as bad as smoking or alcohol; they were addicted. I'm curing them," explained Big Grandma, conveniently forgetting the large doses of literature she indulged in herself.

At that moment Phoebe came charging into the hall, demanding to speak to her mother, and so Big Grandma had no time to explain that almost her only preparation for her granddaughters' visit had been to pack up every one of the several hundred books she owned in cardboard boxes and pile them up in the storeroom above the garage. Graham, who had helped carry out this operation, had been sworn to secrecy, and tastefully arranged pieces from an old dinner service now filled the empty bookshelves. The only things that had been forgotten were the cookery books in the kitchen, but once they had been exhausted her granddaughters had been forced to cease escaping for long and unhelpful periods down their literary boltholes. Lately she had allowed herself to think that her weeks of effort were being rewarded. The long quest for something, anything, to read appeared to be almost forgotten. Not that there wasn't still a long way to go . . .

"Good morning," said Big Grandma, coming into Ruth and Naomi's room early one bright day. "Where's Naomi?"

"Down the garden." Ruth inspected her sweater carefully, found the label that should go at the back, turned it around, and put it on back to front.

"Ruth," said Big Grandma impatiently, "you would make a good ostrich!"

"Why?"

"Just because you personally can no longer see the gravy drips down the front of your sweater does not mean that they are no longer visible!"

"I thought my hair covered them up."

"Just what Lady Godiva said."

"I can't seem to find anything clean," Ruth explained, "except a nightie of Phoebe's."

"Well?"

"Well, it won't fit. Anyway, it would look stupid."

"I didn't mean that. Where are your other clothes?"

Ruth looked around the bedroom. It seemed a bit of a silly question.

"There, mostly," she said. "In that heap."

"If you carried it downstairs," suggested Big Grandma, "and loaded it into the washing machine and switched it on . . ."

Ruth, suddenly inspired, began excitedly groveling under her bed, pulling out garments which she had long given up as hopeless causes.

"On second thought," said Big Grandma, when she saw what was emerging, "just take them downstairs. I've got some other things to sort out. I'll put them all in together."

RACHEL WANDERED aimlessly between the house and the garden, waiting for something to happen to her. She had been trying to make a financial asset of her diary by renting it out to her sisters to read, but they had all very meanly refused to part with their money. Sighing dismally Rachel peered through the kitchen window to see what selfish pleasures Big Grandma was enjoying.

Sorting out the washing! thought Rachel. About time!

Big Grandma looked up, saw Rachel watching, waved a friendly sock, and then carelessly tossed it into the trash can.

"Phoebe, look!" exclaimed Rachel in surprise. "She's throwing our clothes away!"

It was true. Big Grandma had the kitchen trash can propped open on one side of her, and the washing machine door open on the other. From the laundry basket between the two she pulled items of clothing and either tossed them neatly with her left hand into the washing machine, or else flipped them into the can on her right.

"Won't you get into trouble?" shouted Rachel through the glass, but Big Grandma did not seem to hear her question so she went inside to repeat it.

"Who from?" asked Big Grandma, discarding a torn purple nylon T-shirt of Naomi's.

"Mum?" suggested Rachel.

Big Grandma shook the last few socks from the laundry basket into the can, washed her hands, and switched on the machine.

"You needn't worry, Rachel; I'm only throwing rubbish away."

"But we wear them," Rachel pointed out.

"Well, you'll have to wear something else now," said Big Grandma reasonably.

Rachel did not answer. Looking somewhat preoccupied she stared from the washing machine to the cupboard under the sink.

"I hope you won't think I'm intruding," continued Big Grandma politely, "but your mouth and your chin and parts of your nose have gone blue. As have your hands and your wrists."

Rachel peered into the kitchen mirror and stuck out a blue tongue.

"I've been writing," she explained.

Big Grandma smiled her approval. It was nice to see Rachel usefully employed for once. That was one of the results of not allowing them any books to read.

"Naomi gardening?" she asked, wishing to hear further reinforcement of her theory.

"Um," agreed Rachel. "Measuring her lettuces and earthing up radishes, she said."

"Did she?" Well, Big Grandma supposed, measuring lettuces and earthing up radishes, while not intrinsically useful in themselves, showed at least that Naomi had the right idea.

"And Ruth?"

"Ruth's behind the compost heap," said Rachel cautiously. "She's lit a little fire and she's got a little can full of water. . . ."

"Good, good!" said Big Grandma. "That's the spirit!"

Ruth's interesting-bone collection had lately caused some friction. Diligent searching of beach and hill had resulted in an awful abundance of specimens. The latest addition (Donated by: G. Brocklebank) was the head of a not very recently deceased herring gull, and Ruth, at Rachel's suggestion, had endeavored to remove the not inconsiderable amount of herring gull still attached to the skull by boiling it in the kitchen. Less than fragrant odors had rapidly penetrated every room of the house, and Big Grandma in her wrath had cursed natural history in general and Ruth in particular. Nevertheless she was glad to hear that Ruth had withstood her diatribe. Natural history was after all a study to be encouraged.

"And Phoebe is fishing in a bucket," remarked Ruth.

It happened that so far Big Grandma had not beheld this sight, Phoebe having instinctively pursued the sport with some caution. Today, however, she sat in a patch of sunlight clearly visible from the kitchen window. Big Grandma, who could find reason for self-congratulation in having lettuce-measuring and dead-bird-boiling protégées, could by no amount of wishful thinking discover anything praiseworthy in fishing in a bucket. Nor could she bear the sight of such futile occupation.

"Whatever are you doing, Phoebe?" she asked, hurrying outside.

"Fishing," Phoebe dreamily replied.

"Oh well," said Big Grandma, remembering that after all Phoebe was only six. "I suppose it's harmless enough."

"Fishing and thinking," said Phoebe.

"Well, at least you're thinking," said Big Grandma. "That's something, anyway. And far be it from me to ask what thoughts you find so entrancing."

"I'm thinking about money."

"Money?" asked Big Grandma. "At your age? Do you often think about money?"

"Always when I'm fishing," Phoebe told her.

"Then you can just stop fishing at once," ordered Big Grandma firmly, "and come inside with me and I will find something more suitable to occupy your mind!"

Rachel had been wondering as she watched Big Grandma. Suppose she, too, indulged in a little discarding of unwanted items. As soon as she was left alone in the kitchen she burrowed under the kitchen sink, hauled out the three dusty, damp-labeled, ominous cans of dog food, and stowed them away in the trash can, beneath a good deep layer of the family's ex-wardrobe. Then, feeling extremely successful and brave and free forever of the worry of eating dog food, she sauntered off to find her sisters.

RUTH AND NAOMI sat upwind of the unsavory brew in the tin can and glared disapproval at their little sister.

"What have you done?" demanded Ruth, for it was plain that the nonchalant, swaggering Rachel had done something very unusual.

"Chucked away the dog food."

"What if she notices?"

"She won't."

"You said that when you cut your dress up and she did and you told her we made you."

"You're not telling her that this time," said Naomi.

"I don't want to. And I'll tell her myself only I'm waiting till after the trash men come in case she gets the cans back out again."

Such sudden independence was too much to argue with. Ruth and Naomi sat silent.

"You ought to be grateful to me," said Rachel, poking the fire and nearly dislodging the tin can.

"You're not to mess about with fires," remarked Ruth automatically.

"Shall if I like," said Rachel cheerfully. "Why shouldn't I?"

"*Because you're still too young!*" shouted Ruth and Naomi together.

"I'm going," said Rachel, getting to her feet with dignity, "because it smells here!" And she went.

"Good old Rachel," said Ruth, not entirely cheerfully. "Not that Big Grandma would have cooked that stuff, anyway. It was just a joke."

"We've been training Rachel to do something like that for years," answered Naomi, "but it still feels funny now that she has."

"Anyway," said Ruth, looking on the bright side, "it will be nice not to get the blame for everything she does wrong. Go on with what you were saying before she came."

"I've been thinking about that room over the garage. There's only one thing I can think of that she'd bother locking up in there."

"Books?" asked Ruth, who had also been considering the matter.

"That's what I thought. Oh, look! Your can's fallen over!"

Ruth dived through the reeking smoke to rescue the contents of the can. "This isn't going to work," she said, gloomily inspecting them.

"No, and it stinks," said Naomi. "And you've put the fire out. Natural history always sounds nice and clean in books; I don't know why yours always is so disgusting." She poked at the cooling can disparagingly, tipped it sideways, and got herring gull juice all over her plaster cast.

"I don't know what you see in it all," said Naomi.

Alone, Ruth buried Graham's present in the compost heap. Interesting bones had, for the moment at least, lost some of their charm. A proper naturalist, she knew, would be dealing with live animals, and she had seen very few of these. The small garden in the dusty street of the redbrick town where Ruth had spent her life offered very limited opportunities for the amateur naturalist. So far Ruth had seen three dead mice, caught in traps in the shed, one gray squirrel that lived in the school playground, attracted by an unlimited supply of chips and sandwich crusts, several Cumbrian rabbits, and assorted, unremarkable birds.

It was not much of a record. Ruth knew it was not, and was ashamed. It was bad enough for someone who lived in Lincolnshire, but for someone who had spent a summer in Cumbria it was disgraceful. Especially when only a mile or so away from that person lived the oldest and most wonderful of all British animals, the bearlike, panda-faced, earth-dwelling ancient of the countryside, the badger. All Ruth had to do was sit quietly in sight of a set one night, and she would see them.

She wished they didn't only come out at night.

She wished she was not afraid of the dark.

"Come badger-watching with me?" she asked Naomi when she had faced the idea of going alone and turned it down as impossible.

"No thanks!" said Naomi emphatically. "Catch me!"

Ruth approached Phoebe, who was not lacking in courage of the stubborn, pigheaded kind.

"I'm too busy," said Phoebe, who had learned in an afternoon of intensive instruction the game of chess, and who was now engrossed in a book of chess problems.

Rachel agreed to come, but her price was too high.

"I haven't got that much money," said Ruth. "You know I haven't."

"Well, I can't come then," said Rachel.

Toward evening Ruth found herself heading for her last resort, Graham's house. It was all very well Naomi pointing out that since they were living in a more or less haunted house already, she had little to lose by spending the night on a so-far-as-they-knew-ghost-free hill. "Better the devil you know," Big Grandma had remarked when she unscrewed the waste pipe of the kitchen sink to see why the water wouldn't run out. And better the ghost you know, thought Ruth.

The Brocklebanks' kitchen door was standing open and there was a horrible noise coming from inside. It could have been bagpipes, but somehow it was more rasping; there was something horribly violinish about it, and the tune reminded Ruth of a song she didn't like, but she couldn't have said which song it was.

"Do be quiet, Graham," Ruth heard Mrs. Brocklebank say. "I can't hear myself think!"

Ruth knocked at the open door, but nobody heard her. Mrs. Brocklebank was ironing a great heap of screwed-up blue denim. Graham's grandad was sitting at the table rattling a pair of teaspoons. Graham was astride a chair the wrong way around, bright red in the face, and blowing and blowing into a large mouth organ. His eyes were shut tight.

"We are the music makers," shouted Graham's grandad when he saw Ruth in the doorway. "That's poetry, that is, but you wouldn't know. You wouldn't know how to play the spoons either, I doubt?"

Graham's mother clouted Graham across the head with a pair of trousers and he opened his eyes and stopped blowing. "Come in, Ruth," she called, "and I hope you've come to take him away! Goodness knows we're not musical in this house, but that mouth organ is more than flesh and blood can stand!"

"Sweet music," Graham's grandad remarked, "though I like a nice brass band myself!"

"Hello," said Graham, busily shaking the spit out of his mouth organ. "Did you know what I was playing?"

"Sort of," Ruth admitted, "I recognized it but I couldn't remember the name."

"See," said Graham to his mother, "I told you it was a real tune! 'Amazin' Grace'!"

"Oh, yes."

"Beautiful!" Graham's grandad shouted. "Amazin' bloody Grace! You should learn 'Moonlight and Roses,' and then I could sing along! 'Moonlight and roweses,' " he wailed in his loud, flat, tractor-engine-drowning voice, " 'Reminds me, a yew!' and lass can play the spoons!"

While they quieted Graham's grandad, who insisted on playing the spoons all over his body (as, he said, he had once seen a stark naked sailor do in Calcutta before the war) Ruth explained about the badger-watching and how she didn't really want to go by herself.

"I can't come," said Graham. "I'm busy!"

"Busy nothing," said Mrs. Brocklebank, "of course you can go. If I don't have some quiet my head will split. And you can walk your grandad back to his cottage on the way."

"I 'ent ready to go yet," said Graham's grandad.

"Neither am I," said Graham.

"I'm 'avin' a cup of tea first."

"So'm I," said Graham.

However, they did finally set off only an hour later, Ruth carrying a basket full of provisions for Graham's grandad to take home, Graham sulking and slashing at the grasses along the way with his grandfather's walking stick. Already the colors of the sunlight were fading from the fields.

Graham's grandad's cottage stood at the far side of the village, on the road up to Big Grandma's house. It was his habit to stop at the farm with his daughter and her family until he couldn't bear their fussing and worrying any longer and left for his own house. After a few days alone he would get bored and feel the need to aggravate somebody again, and then he would move back to the farm. The only thing that slightly marred his old age was that everyone in his family, in the whole village for that matter, had heard time and again the stories he was so fond of telling, and irreverently took them all with about a shovelful of salt. Ruth didn't though. The lass didn't know any better.

"See that track running round fell and up ower top-side?" he asked. "Know what we call that? Corpse pad!"

He waited for Ruth to digest this information.

"Why?"

"When this village didn't 'ave no churchyard corpses was took up that track for burrying in the village ower the way. They 'ad their churchyard, see? 'Course," he added thoughtfully, stopping to gaze over a gate at a flock of curly-horned sheep, "course you could burry a corpse where you liked in them days. Nobody said nowt. Folks used to like a churchyard though."

Graham took out his mouth organ and, sitting on the gate, began to play his unholy version of "Amazing Grace."

"How'd they get the . . . dead people up there?" asked Ruth. "It's very steep."

"Strap the coffin on a pony's back," explained Graham's grandad.

Ruth thought of a coffin strapped on a pony's back. Surely it would stick out over the tail.

"Longways or crossways?"

"Crossways," answered Graham's grandad, somewhat surprised at such a sensible question. "Ponies 'ated the job. Knew what they were carrying. Run off, some of them, coffin and all.

"Never come back, some of 'em," he went on. "Some folks reckon they're still there. See 'em wandering about at nights, like, still strapped to the coffin!"

Graham had stopped playing and was listening to the story. He glanced up at the hill, and looked across at Ruth, but he did not say anything. Neither did Ruth. The three of them turned and continued walking toward the village. Graham's grandad was talking about badgers now. He was telling Ruth about a day, seventy something years ago, when he'd been only a lad. He'd been sent out to the hen house one evening to see what the hens were making such a fuss about. Graham's grandad had opened the door very quietly to catch whatever it was unawares, and he'd seen two badgers. "One lay on its back in middle of the floor, while t'other were bringing eggs in 'is mouth and piling them up on 'is mate's belly!

"Great big 'eap there was piled up," Graham's grandad continued.

"Gets bigger every time he tells it," Graham said aside to Ruth.

"Great big 'eap of eggs! Dozens! What about that, then?"

"What happened?" asked Ruth.

"In finish," Graham's grandad said, "badger on floor said 'twere enough. . . ."

"Said it?" shouted Graham in triumph. "You never said they could talk before!"

"Never said they could now!" Graham's grandad bellowed. "I know what I see though! When 'twere enough badger that were collecting eggs cop 'old of t'other and pulled 'im away! Pulled 'im clean through the 'ole they dug to get in!"

"What did you do?"

"I stood staring a bit and then I run off for me dad but by the time 'e come back with the gun badgers were gone, eggs were gone, nowt left but the 'ole! Badgers is clever!"

"Certainly are," commented Graham, "not many animals can talk!"

His grandad ignored him. "Knew some badgers once," he said. "Great fat ones they was . . ." and off he rambled with another story.

It was slow work, walking along with Graham's grandad. He couldn't pass a field without stopping to look in it, and everyone they met halted to speak for a minute. The light was becoming grayer and grayer, and the top of the hill was hidden in a swirl of cloud.

"I'll not climb it agen," Graham's grandad said, looking up at it. "I done my share of climbing. Used to race to the top we did, running. Been up it in all weathers."

"Snow?" asked Ruth.

"Snow?" Graham's grandad spat. "Snow, 'ail, 'urry-cane, blizzard. Two weeks of blizzard we 'ad once, and I climbed it every day. 'Arf the village did."

"A plane crashed up there," Graham told Ruth. "They saw it against the snow, and they could see people moving about but then a blizzard came."

"Who's telling?" asked Graham's grandad crossly. "I am! Blizzard came and when we'd waited and they never come we went to look for them. Thought they might have got a bit of shelter among the rocks or summat. Folks were up there looking every day."

"Did you find them?"

"Two weeks later. Froze stiff. Terrible. They'd tried to crawl down. Should have stayed with the plane, we'd have found them a lot sooner. Too late by the time we did."

They had reached Graham's grandad's house at last. He stood by the gate, looking up at the hill.

"Good luck to you," he said. "You'd not get me on fell at night. And if you don't believe what I've told you, you ask your gran. Many a thing I've told her that no one else believe and she's said, aye, she read of someat like that or whatever. She've a grand collection of books. You've no call to stay ignorant while you live up there!"

He took his basket of food from Ruth and his stick from Graham and opened the gate. "I'll not ask you in," he said. "You'll want to be away. I 'ope you see nowt of them ponies."

They watched him go in and close the door. A light was switched on inside and shone through the window into the garden.

"So do I," said Graham gloomily.

"So do you what?" Ruth brought her thoughts back from Big Grandma's books to the present problems.

"Hope we see nowt of them ponies."

It was already only too obvious to Ruth that they were not going to see anything of the badgers that night. The hill seemed full of coffin-laden ponies and crawling corpses.

"Scared?"

"Nope."

"Oh, well, I am. I'm not going."

Graham sighed with relief.

" 'Spose," said Ruth, taking full advantage of the moment of companionship between them, "she told you not to tell us anything about her books?"

Graham grinned.

"And she's stuck them in that little room over the garage to stop us getting them?" pursued Ruth.

"Surprised it stopped you," remarked Graham.

"She's got it locked."

"Surprised that stopped you, too," said Graham. "Anyway, I'm going to get off back before it gets any darker. Or," he added most heroically, "do you want me to take you home first?"

Highly offended, Ruth declined his offer and set off at a run for the comforting, only slightly haunted shelter of Big Grandma's house. Graham sighed with relief again and turned toward the village. Through the window Graham's grandad watched them go their separate ways. Then he switched on his electric fire and turned up the television so that all the people were shouting at each other. It had been a good day, he thought, and he had a delicious feeling of having stirred up a bit of trouble there at the end. It made him feel young somehow.

Chapter 13

"GRAHAM ADMITTED IT," reported Ruth. "They've been there all summer. Even if we got in now, we'd never have time to read every one. We're going home in less than two weeks."

"Much less than two weeks," interrupted Naomi, counting days on the kitchen calendar.

"What d'you mean, going home?" asked Phoebe, exercising as usual her amazing ability of discounting basic facts of life. "I'm not. Not until I've seen Big Grandma's books, anyway."

"Neither am I," agreed the new, independent (sometimes) Rachel. "And I want to go back to the cave and see where Naomi fell off."

"Thanks very much!"

"And where she was sick on her foot," continued Rachel, "and I want to go and see Mrs. Brocklebank again. She said I could."

"I haven't seen the badgers yet."

"I haven't dug that bit where the cabbages were."

"How could you with a broken arm?"

"I could if I wanted to."

"We ought to get her good-bye presents," said Ruth. "After all, she hasn't been that bad. Except about the books. D'you think we could manage to get a look at them before we go? Just to see what we've been missing?"

"We'll never have time to get everything done." Naomi was still studying the calendar. "And I've got to go back to that beastly awful hospital the day before we go, to get my arm checked. Graham might have told us earlier about the books. We could have arranged something if we'd had a bit more time."

"What sort of thing?"

"P'raps we could've picked the lock. We could've bought tools if we'd known. Too late now; we've spent all our money."

"We don't know how to pick locks, anyway, so what use would they have been?"

"Obviously," Naomi was withering, "obviously you get instructions with them when you buy them. Anyway, it's too late now."

"We ought to climb the hill once more."

"And make another bonfire and cook dinner."

"We could invite Big Grandma."

"My lettuces and radishes are still too small. They'll never be ready before we go."

"I'll never have time to swim to the Isle of Man now. We ought to start doing things much faster."

THE LAST DAYS of the holiday, like fairy gold counted in the sunlight, disappeared as fast as they were numbered. The shining wealth of summer that had been theirs to squander dwindled to a few dull-gleaming days. Ruth, Naomi, Rachel, and Phoebe began to spend them with the distraught recklessness of those who see the end of the world. A day was ransomed to climb the hill, and a morning to revisit the scene of Naomi's accident.

"Which one did you fall off?" Naomi watched hopefully as her sisters and Graham climbed up, ran down, stood on the step from which she had fallen, closed their eyes, let go of the rock, did it backward, stood on one leg, tickled Rachel, shoved Phoebe, tried to startle Graham into jumping, and distracted Ruth with imaginary badgers. It was as they had imagined, impossible to fall. They marveled.

"Look, I'm doing it on tiptoe, leaning outward, with my eyes crossed. Tell me a joke, someone!"

"Oh, come down," said Naomi crossly. "I'll show you where I was sick."

"Looks like any other grass to me," said Rachel, disappointed.

"Now, if we run all the way back," said Ruth, "we'll have time to go swimming before lunch."

"BIG GRANDMA," said Ruth, one desperate evening, "will you come badger-watching with me?"

"Certainly," agreed Big Grandma cordially, "nothing I'd rather do."

Three evenings later there was a sound in the bracken and a glimpse of black and white in the moonlight.

"Was it worth it?" asked Big Grandma as they tiptoed home.

"A thousand times," said Ruth. At that moment of happiness, if Ruth hadn't been Ruth, and Big Grandma hadn't been Big Grandma, they might have hugged each other, but instead they exchanged a brief, smiling glance. Ruth wondered, slightly guiltily, if, in view of Big Grandma's kindness, she ought still to be plotting to raid her books, and decided she should. Big Grandma wondered, also slightly guiltily, if, in view of Ruth's shining-eyed gratitude, she ought to hand over her library, and decided she shouldn't.

"BIG GRANDMA came badger-watching with me," Ruth told Graham the next day. "We saw them twice! Twice! You should have come."

"Oh yes?" said Graham skeptically. "I think your gran must be cracking up at last."

"Why didn't you come to lunch yesterday? I told your mum to ask you specially," Rachel demanded. "We cooked it on the beach again."

"That's why I didn't come," said Graham.

"It was good," Rachel told him. "Big Grandma drove us down with all the stuff so we didn't have to carry it."

"She sat on a cushion," put in Phoebe, "and ate everything we cooked and said it was lovely."

"What did you do for her?"

"Scrambled eggs and sardines and stewed plums. And we bought it with our own money."

"Crikey!" said Graham. "She *must* be cracking up!"

"Two more days left," said Naomi one morning, and the thought was so dreadful that they changed it to forty-eight hours instead.

"Time to do ninety-six short things," said Ruth.

"How long will it take you to pack those bones?" demanded Naomi.

Ruth, who between cutting the grass and painting a farewell picture of a badger for Big Grandma, was trying to reduce three large shopping bags which she could not lift, into one small bag that she could, without abandoning any of the contents, shook her head and said she did not know.

"Well, hurry up! Have you seen if that door's still locked?" For several days the girls had, at every available opportunity, sneaked through Big Grandma's bedroom to test the lock of the storeroom door.

"Tried it about an hour ago."

Naomi sighed and stared critically at Ruth's picture. "Why are you painting it, anyway? She doesn't like things like that. Think of that whole box of ornaments she gave to Graham for his shooting practice."

"She'll like this." Ruth put down her brush to ram a handful of loose vertebrae into a skull. "What are you giving her? Have you thought of anything?"

"There's something I've got to do for a good-bye present," said Naomi cautiously, "but I won't be able to tell you what it is until I've done it."

"Why not?"

In case I can't, thought Naomi. "What about my lettuces and radishes?" she asked aloud.

"What about them?"

"Nothing," said Naomi sadly. She had given up the daily drenching of their roots with Baby Bio. It seemed to make no difference. Instead she turned her attention to the rough patch of ground where the cabbages had been. The earth was all weedy and lumpy looking, and she remembered the night before she had broken her arm when Big Grandma had said, "I wish I could dig over that patch where the cabbages were," and she regretted not having returned that night and dug it in the dark. Now Graham would do it, when they were gone, and perhaps Big Grandma would say, "I thought Naomi might do that, but of course she couldn't, not with a broken arm." Then Naomi, who had so far always contrived to carry out Big Grandma's gardening challenges, would have failed.

THERE WAS a scholarly group gathered beneath the damson tree. Rachel, seated as if for inspiration on a stack of Shakespeare (*Histories and Poems, Tragedies and Romances, Comedies*), was editing and amending her diary, which she had finally decided to bestow on Big Grandma.

"Will you miss me when I'm gone?" she asked Big Grandma.

Big Grandma paused and put down the potato she was peeling, made a move on the chessboard that stood between herself and Phoebe, checked the amount of peas her opponent had shelled, and answered, "Possibly."

Naomi arrived to say, with a definite note of panic in her voice, "It's only forty and a half more hours now. This time next week do you know where we'll be? This time the day after tomorrow we'll be nearly back. It's half past three. It'll be dark in less than five hours and there won't be time to do anything tomorrow, I've got to go to the hospital. How can you all just sit there? Don't you know how fast it's going. . . ."

"Naomi, stop!" commanded Big Grandma.

"And there's still something I've got to do," said Naomi, and she gazed worriedly down the garden.

EVENING CAME WITH a sunset of flame and scarlet over the sea. Big Grandma, thinking it might be calming, drove them down to the beach to watch it. The sky was fire colored in the west, pale green overhead, and blue with stars in it above the hills. "This time in two days' time," said Rachel mournfully, "Mum will be trying to make us go to bed."

"In our new pale pink bedrooms," added Phoebe, remembering the latest phone call from Lincolnshire. "My most unfavorite color."

"Pale pink bedrooms," repeated Big Grandma callously, "which will just match your pale pink cowardly little characters. What's happened to your courage? Packed it?"

PALE PINK COWARDLY little characters, thought Naomi, alone and watchful in the middle of the night, and she got out of bed.

"What are you doing?" whispered Ruth across the dark.

"Nothing. D'you think Big Grandma's asleep?"

"I heard her come up half an hour ago. Why? Why are you getting dressed?"

"Ssssh."

"Tell me where you're going."

"You wouldn't understand," said Naomi, who did not quite understand herself. "Anyway, I haven't got time. Not far."

"How far?"

"Just to the garden if you must know." Naomi opened the bedroom door and peered cautiously out. All the lights were switched off, and except for the sound of Big Grandma's windy breathing the house seemed quiet.

"Bye," whispered Naomi, and padded in her socks down the stairs. In the kitchen she pulled on a pair of Big Grandma's wellington boots, found the flashlight that was kept beside the fuse box, wrapped her plaster cast in a shopping bag, and went out into the black, waiting garden. By flashlight she chose the largest spade in the garden shed.

IT WAS ASTONISHINGLY difficult. Naomi had been prepared for hard work, and perhaps a certain amount of awkwardness, but she had never thought it might be actually impossible. For a start her flashlight kept falling over. It wouldn't stand so that it shone on the bit she was trying to dig, and she didn't think she could dig in the dark. And, anyway, it was difficult to dig with a broken arm. First you balance the spade on the bit you want to cut. Then you tread on it with one foot, to get it stuck firmly into the ground. Then, keeping your plaster cast out of the way of hitting the spade handle, you jump on top of the spade, so as to press it right in. After that you stand on the ground and lean on the handle to lift up the spadeful of soil. Then with your good arm low down on the shaft, and your broken one across the top to balance it, you raise the spadeful, turn it over, and drop the soil into the same space again.

That is one dig.

Naomi dug one dig and she thought she might as well give up. After five more spadefuls she thought perhaps she was getting the hang of it, and then, after a few more she decided she wasn't after all, and what was worse, she fully expected to break her arm again any minute. But she still went on digging.

By the time Ruth found her she had dug a row and a half and had just finished calculating that there were probably eighteen and a half still to go.

"You look awful—all hunched up in the light from the flashlight swearing and cursing," said Ruth.

"Go away."

"Look at those slugs and worms coming out," remarked Ruth. "I bet they're hypnotized by the light."

Naomi, ignoring her, painfully and slowly finished the row.

"Shall I hold the flashlight?"

"That's right," said Naomi bitterly, "you do a bit of work, too. I'll dig and dig with my broken arm and everything and you stand there and hold the flashlight."

"All right," said Ruth.

For a long time Ruth stood in the empty night, shining the light on the edge of Naomi's spade.

"Seventeen and a half to go," said Naomi a long time later when she had discarded the shopping bag around her cast as being much too clumsy to work with.

"Nearer thirty," said Ruth.

Naomi moved the spade one width along the row,

balanced it, stepped on it, jumped on the top, heaved up the earth, and turned it over. "Thirty!" she said. "It can't be!"

"Stop and work it out yourself."

"I can't stop."

Slowly the glow of the flashlight traced Naomi's weary progress to the end of the row.

"Let me have a turn."

"No. It's my good-bye present. I've got to do it."

"It's freezing just standing here."

"Well, go in, then," said Naomi beginning another row.

For a long time the garden was quiet except for the wind in the ash tree, and the squelch and tumble of Naomi's spade. Suddenly the circle of light wavered wildly and shot over the garden.

"Hold it steady."

"I think I fell asleep."

"Go in, then."

"All right."

Naomi found herself alone and furious with the hopeless flashlight. Coward! she thought. Coward and traitor! I'd have stayed with you!

She was so angry she forgot how tired she was. She forgot to move the light. She dug in the dark, thinking of Ruth warm in bed, while her sister toiled alone in the miserable Cumbrian wind, in the pitch-dark, miserable, Cumbrian garden.

The row was finished, and the next, without Naomi noticing them pass. All her thoughts were taken up with Ruth. It would have been better if she'd never come down at all, rather than come to abandon her broken-armed sister in her time of need.

"Cup of tea!"

There was Ruth, standing on the path, dressed in all she possessed, holding a mug of tea in each hand.

"Tea?" asked Naomi, limp with gratitude. "I thought you'd gone back to bed."

The tea was boiling hot, thick with tea leaves, and very sweet. Ruth had poured it into the two pewter mugs that usually stood on the mantlepiece in the kitchen. They held a pint each, which was why she had chosen them. Both were very dusty and there happened to be a stray button in the bottom of Naomi's, but such trifles presented no problems in the dark.

"I feel like I've come alive again," said Naomi, tipping the dregs and the button out onto the ground and picking up the spade.

"Shall I do a bit?"

"No thanks."

"I'll hold the light, then."

"Okay. What time was it when you came out?"

"Half-past twelve."

Slowly, but certainly, they could just see that the patch of turned earth was widening. After a long, long time Naomi asked, "Do you think I've done a third yet?"

"Easily. More like half. Let me do a bit."

"No thanks," said Naomi, digging like clockwork, hardly feeling her arms or legs or stiffening back. She had passed the stage of aching.

"Cold?" she asked Ruth deeper in the night when she could look back and know she was more than halfway.

"I've got a hot water bottle up my sweater."

Naomi dug on. Once again the flashlight skidded across the garden and she heard Ruth stumble on the path.

Then Ruth woke up again and held the light steady.

"You've nearly finished," she said in surprise to Naomi. "I didn't notice how far you'd got."

"I'm trying not to look behind me."

Spadefuls of night inched slowly through the garden.

"Last row," said Naomi.

Ruth held the light ceremoniously high.

"WHAT'S THE time?"

"Five to three."

They crept through the kitchen and upstairs, crawled out of their clothes, and fell, unwashed, into bed and sleep.

THE LAST DAY dawned bright and horrifying.

"How many hours now?" asked Rachel at breakfast, a melancholy meal of porridge and sardines, well suited to the depression of the day.

"Twenty-six."

"Had we better start turning them into minutes?"

"I don't think so."

"This is the unhappiest day of my life," said Rachel.

"You haven't had it yet," replied Big Grandma impatiently.

"I have a premo-what's-its-name, when you can tell something's going to happen before you start," explained Rachel, and later on she was to say to her sisters,

"You'll never ignore my premo-what's-its-name again!" ("We will," said Naomi in reply.)

Big Grandma, preoccupied with packing and train times, seemed not to notice the traces of the night's happenings, tea leaves in the pewter mugs and tired grandchildren. Mrs. Conroy was to meet the girls at Crewe, where they would change trains, and Big Grandma did not approve of this.

"They're perfectly capable of making the journey alone," she told Mrs. Conroy, but Mrs. Conroy replied that they were perfectly capable of anything, and therefore she would be happier meeting them.

"Fancy having to waste half the day at the hospital," grumbled Naomi.

"Good gracious, I'd forgotten!" exclaimed Big Grandma. "How on earth did you get that plaster cast into such a disgusting state?"

"We've got to be back in time for going to supper with Graham as well," Naomi reminded her, ignoring the question of her plaster cast.

"The good-riddance supper," said Rachel.

Phoebe alone did not join in the conversation, sitting remote and preoccupied at the end of the table, staring into her bowl of porridge and brown sugar. A sardine was lying in solitary state on the top.

"Hurry up, Phoebe," urged Big Grandma. "You put it there so you can eat it!"

"What's the matter with you?" asked her sisters, noticing her unusual quietness for the first time.

"Nothing," said Phoebe, tranquilly eating the sardine with the face of one who sees visions.

"Something's the matter with Phoebe," said Ruth as they sat in the garden later that morning. "She's stopped reading chess problems and she's stopped fishing in a bucket. She just walks around smiling."

"Who cares?" asked Naomi. "You know she doesn't live in the same world as everyone else. D'you know she's started talking about her Christmas-list money again? Offered me twenty pence when we got home to wash her some socks yesterday. I sometimes think Graham's right when he says . . ."

"What?"

"She's cracked," continued Naomi. "Anyway, go on writing. Put, 'You have bent my elbow too much; you have put the plaster on too tight; you have put it on too high; you have put it on too thick so it is very hot and itches.' "

"Is it drying yet?" asked Big Grandma.

"Not too bad."

Big Grandma had resourcefully cleaned up the cast with a bit of paint left over from the kitchen walls. It was now white (with a touch of apple green) and Naomi, clad only in her swimsuit (until the paint dried), was dictating a list of complaints that she intended presenting to the doctor when she met him that afternoon.

" 'Very hot and itches,' " repeated Ruth, scribbling away.

" 'It is not properly waterproof; it is coming to bits at the ends; white is not a good color for plaster casts; I do not think you have set the bones straight.' "

"Don't say that," advised Ruth, "in case he breaks it and sets it again."

"Skip it then, go on to the waiting. Put, 'I had to wait too long to see you; the waiting room is very boring; the painkillers you gave me did not work very well; I think it should have mended by now.' That's all."

"What about his stupid jokes and what you thought about the nurse and not getting an ambulance?" suggested Ruth.

"I don't want to make him angry," pointed out Naomi. "I'll just read that list out politely to him and leave it on his desk when I go so that he can look at it whenever he needs to."

"What rare and graceful tact," commented Big Grandma, who was torn between the desire to see the doctor's reaction when Naomi presented her document and a more prudent (but less exciting) instinct to remain discreetly in the waiting room.

The cast was dry by midmorning.

"It looks quite nice," said Ruth, "except where that egg mark keeps showing through."

"Good-bye," said Rachel, coming up to them and going away again.

"Good-bye," said Big Grandma. "Come back! Where are you going?"

"To see Mrs. Brocklebank."

"Now?"

"Before lunch. She said I could go when I liked."

"That doesn't mean you can turn up for every meal," Naomi pointed out.

"Quite so," agreed Big Grandma. "You can go when you've had your lunch here, but not before, and I'm sure she'll be busy this afternoon as it is, so don't outstay your welcome there."

"What's that?"

"When they say, 'They're going to be missing you at home,'" explained Naomi, "and ask if you've said you're going to be away so long, and take you outside and show you the front garden."

"Why?"

"To get you out of the house."

"Why'd they want to do that?" asked Rachel, completely confused.

"Because they're sick of you and they want you to clear off," explained Ruth, "but they're too polite to say so."

"Oh, it's a waste of time trying to teach Rachel manners," remarked Naomi.

"We'll have to do it someday."

"I've got manners," said Rachel belligerently.

"All right, you've got manners," agreed Ruth. "Just not very good ones. Why didn't you finish getting dressed this morning?"

"I am dressed."

Ruth and Naomi looked wearily at each other and Naomi explained: "That was manners for, 'Why didn't you get washed?'"

"And brush your hair," added Ruth.

"And tie it with another ribbon," said Naomi. "You've chewed all the color out of the ends of that one."

"And tuck your T-shirt in, or leave it out, one or the other."

"And clean your teeth."

"I've cleaned them," said Rachel triumphantly.

"That's right," encouraged Big Grandma, "you stick

up for yourself! I've never known toothpaste vanish the way it does in this house!"

At this remark Rachel disappeared guiltily upstairs. She had a very private game in which toothpaste was not toothpaste, but peppermint cream. She ate quite a lot of peppermint cream toothpaste during the night.

I t w a s a lonely afternoon for Ruth, with Naomi at the hospital and Rachel scraping out cake bowls with Mrs. Brocklebank. Phoebe had disappeared soon after Big Grandma had driven away. Like an aimless daylight ghost Ruth wandered the empty house saying her good-byes to the old-fashioned rooms, the views from the windows, the grandfather clock with the sea gull-painted face, stopped for a quarter of a century at five past nine.

"Not a very restful time for it to stop at," Naomi had once remarked, and, "Would you like me to mend your clock?" Ruth had asked.

"Not at all, I like it how it is," Big Grandma had replied.

"But it doesn't tick."

"It does when I want it to," and Big Grandma had swung the pendulum to make the old clock tick.

"She likes to control everything," Naomi had grumbled. "Even the time."

Ruth, passing the clock and patting it in farewell, remembered the conversation, and how Big Grandma had glared at Naomi and said, almost defensively, "Anyway, some of its insides are missing!"

"None of our insides are missing," Phoebe had remarked cryptically.

Rachel's return from the Brocklebanks' was marked by the familiar crash of falling china as she ferreted through the larder for something to eat.

"Do you know where Phoebe is?" asked Ruth, running downstairs from Big Grandma's bedroom where she had been saying a wistful good-bye to the locked storeroom door. "What have you been crying about?"

"Nothing," said Rachel. "Anyway, I haven't. What have you been crying about?"

"Nothing. That door's still locked—I've just checked. And I've tried picking the lock like Naomi said, but it only bends the screwdriver."

"Perhaps there's something in the shed we could use," suggested Rachel hopefully.

Ready to try anything, they set off to ransack the garden shed and there discovered Phoebe. She was sitting on an upturned bucket, a large book open across her knees, and a large, complacent smile across her face. Here was one Conroy at least who had not been crying.

"Where did you get that book?"

They seized it from her and examined it: *The Little Bookroom.* "Mary, with love from Mother," was written inside.

"I haven't seen this before!"

"It must have been Mum's!" and "How did you get in there?" demanded Ruth fiercely, for it was perfectly plain where the book had come from.

"Found the key!"

"How? Why didn't you tell us?"

Phoebe was beginning to look extremely uncomfortable. "I was going to tell you."

With great difficulty they dragged the story from their disgraceful little sister. Even Rachel was shocked.

"Spying through keyholes," declared Ruth, "is disgusting! You know it is!"

"It was only till I saw where she put the key. I knew she must lock it up at night; she was reading in bed once when I went to the bathroom and the book wasn't there in the morning. I couldn't help it. I wanted to see the books. I couldn't think of any undisgusting ways!"

"Where's the key now?"

"In her glasses case."

"Come on"—Ruth and Rachel were running back up the garden path to the house—"we've just got time for a look before they get back!"

"I thought you said it was disgusting!" Phoebe arrived panting in Big Grandma's bedroom as Ruth fitted the key in the lock.

"Well, it's too late now, you've done it." Ruth pushed open the door and they fell down a step into a shadowy room, lit only by one small window which was half obscured by piled boxes. The walls were the same raw pine and concrete block as the garage below, and the floor was rough bare planks, but the books—stacked in heaps and overflowing boxes, a few scattered, open and face-downward—the books were a wealth and glory. They had time for one awed glance around, and then the sound of Big Grandma's car engine sent them flying back into the bedroom, where they replaced the key and skidded down the stairs to saunter as casually as they could to meet the travelers. Fortunately, Big Grandma and Naomi were in such high spirits, having utterly vanquished Naomi's doctor with the list of complaints, that they noticed nothing unusual about the others.

"He didn't say anything," Naomi told Ruth as they changed to go to Graham's good-riddance supper. "He just sat there with his mouth opening and shutting. I think he was ashamed. What's the matter with you?"

"Last night," began Ruth, and explained what Phoebe had seen that night.

"I thought I heard someone creaking about!" exclaimed Naomi, "while I was waiting to get up to do the digging! Go on, then what?" and her face grew more and more dismal as Ruth related the events of the afternoon.

"We only had time to just look in before you came back. There must be hundreds."

"And we're going tomorrow!"

"Yes." In the excitements of the afternoon the girls had almost forgotten it.

"It's not just the books," said Ruth, "it's everything."

"I'm too sad to eat," Rachel told Mrs. Brocklebank at suppertime. Graham looked astonished and Big Grandma burst out laughing.

"Try just nibbling, then," suggested Mrs. Brocklebank kindly, and Rachel, with great courage, nibbled her way through three slices of cheese and mushroom pie, several ham sandwiches, chocolate mousse, and lemon cake.

They talked about the summer and when they would come back.

"Never," said Ruth dolefully. "Not unless Mum and Dad get another five thousand pounds from somewhere."

"Why are you all so fed up?" asked Graham. "In trouble?"

"We've only got fourteen and a half more hours," Rachel explained.

"You can eat a fair bit in fourteen and a half hours," said Graham callously.

"Graham's going to miss you," said Mrs. Brocklebank.

"I'm not," said Graham going bright, bright red.

"Well, I'll be coming back to marry him, anyway," said Rachel, the prospect of which depressed Graham (who had been unaware of his fate) into absolute silence.

"BED, BED, BED," said Big Grandma when they got back, but she was interrupted.

"We were going to give you our good-bye presents," said Ruth, "in case there's no time in the morning."

"Presents?" asked Big Grandma.

"Because we've had a nice time," explained Rachel, "even with nothing to read."

Big Grandma did not even flicker at this hint. "Well, let's get at these presents," she said cheerfully.

The parcels, carefully wrapped in birthday paper bought with the last of Ruth's swimming-to-the-Isle-of-Man money ("Good job I didn't go," she had said), stood waiting for Big Grandma on the kitchen table.

There was a spare chessboard from Phoebe, cheerfully, if unconventionally checkered in green and yellow, and a note with it saying, "I hav rit som more chess in the bak of yor book."

A watercolor of a badger, most lovingly painted and

framed in cardboard. Big Grandma gazed at it in astonishment; she had been completely unaware of the fact that Ruth could paint.

A battered and greasy notebook, the meticulous record of a summer's good eating, right up to date with Chapter Forty-One: The Good-Riddance Supper.

"That's what you were scribbling at under the table!" exclaimed Big Grandma. "Big Grandma," she read on the very last page, "you are a very good cook."

"Thank you, Rachel," said Big Grandma.

There were no more presents, but there was a piece of paper which said, "Mine is down the garden. I hope it is all right. Love Naomi." Big Grandma went outside and viewed, by the dwindling light from the flashlight, Naomi's good-bye present. She stayed there a long time and when she came back she said, "My heavens, Naomi!"

And then she made them go to bed. Pausing on the stairs, Ruth gave her one last chance.

"Aren't there any books we could borrow just for tonight, just to help us get to sleep because it's so awful?"

But Big Grandma had held out for too long to mellow all at once.

"Get out the Shakespeare," she suggested cheerfully. "That'll send you off!"

THERE WAS a desperate meeting in Ruth and Naomi's room.

"We can't possibly go without looking."

"No."

"I almost wish we hadn't found where the key was."

"You made me tell you," said Phoebe.

"Don't you ever, ever spy through keyholes again."

"Anyway, what are we going to do? D'you think we could creep in? Just to look?"

"When she's asleep? We couldn't put a light on."

"There isn't one, anyway," said Phoebe. "I looked before."

"The flashlight battery is nearly dead from last night. Are there any candles left from when we went to the cave?"

"There's three in the red handbag under my bed. I was saving them to take home."

"Matches?"

"I've got matches," said Ruth.

"It's lucky she sleeps so heavily." Naomi had already made full use of this fact several times that holiday.

"That's because of her bedtime whiskey," said Phoebe.

"So when she's asleep . . ." said Ruth.

"We'll scratch on your door. We won't light the candles until we get in. We'll have to find the key in the dark. Phoebe can do that, she's seen it before."

"What if she wakes up?"

"We'll just have to explain."

"Its a funny way to spend the last night," whispered Ruth as she and Naomi slid out of bed.

"No funnier than last night was really. I can hear her snoring. You get the key while I fetch the other two. Have you got those matches?"

A few minutes later a goblin procession passed silently through Big Grandma's bedroom: three scraggy forms, clad in tattered pale clothing following the beckoning finger of a small and quaking figure outlined against a dark doorway. Once inside, they pushed the door silently behind them until it almost closed, and stood with thumping hearts until the steady sound of Big Grandma's snoring gave them courage enough to light the candles and begin the exploration.

For a long time ("It must have been hours," said Rachel the next day), they crouched in the flickering candlelight, soundlessly unpacking and repacking the boxes of forbidden books.

"Natural history!" exclaimed Ruth to herself. "Two whole boxes!" Many of the books were old, with gold-edged pages and black-and-white engravings. Beautiful! thought Ruth. I could have tried to copy them. And there were several new ones, full of photographs, the sort of books that Ruth had often pored over in bookshops and at last reluctantly returned to the shelves when the assistant glared too hard.

Naomi, haloed like an angel in the golden light of her candle, was wandering through Big Grandma's collection of local history, looking up places she knew and had heard of, and discovering old churches and stone circles that she might have visited if she had known of them in time. Phoebe, sharing her candle and half asleep, turned page after page of storybooks that had belonged, some to her mother and some to Uncle Robert. Occasionally their names were in the front, together with long addresses, which ended with: Planet Earth, The Milky

Way, Space. Phoebe remembered the delight with which Ruth and Naomi had conjured up the very same address, and marveled that her mother and uncle had thought of it, too.

Rachel, in the darkest corner of the room, rifled through comics more than thirty years old, comics with names she had never heard of and prices she could not believe. Gradually she became aware of a change about her, and looking up, saw her sisters staring at each other with tense, listening faces and wide-open eyes. Big Grandma had stopped snoring.

There was a long pause of frozen stillness, and then they heard her turn in bed, and the snoring begin again, but their nerve was broken, and with silent panic they put down their books, crept on stiff and aching legs to the door, and scurried in fright back to their beds.

"Did she hear us?" whispered Rachel.

"No. She's still asleep. Go to sleep yourself."

"What about the door?"

"I think Ruth closed it," whispered Naomi, pushing her little sisters into bed before departing, completely exhausted by the activities of the last two days and nights.

"Are you asleep?" she whispered to Ruth as she crawled beneath the bedclothes, but Ruth, still clutching the key to the storeroom door, was already too near dreaming to bother answering. Naomi pushed her head under her pillow and tried to forget her sins, and was soon lost in a nightmare where she had to dig the cabbage patch all over again, and it took even longer than the first time.

Chapter 14

‹‹‹‹‹‹‹‹‹‹‹‹‹‹‹‹‹‹‹‹‹‹‹‹‹

RUTH WOKE, as she quite often did, to find herself sitting bolt upright, staring into the first gray light of dawn, cold with fear from some slow-fading dream. There was a pain in her right hand, and looking down she realized for the first time that she was gripping something hard. The storeroom key. She had forgotten they had ever been there, but now memory returned to her. How many hours had she been asleep, she wondered. It was still almost dark, but it would soon be morning she supposed. And it was the last morning; tonight they would be back in Lincolnshire, hundreds of miles from the hills and running streams and seascapes of Cumbria. Ruth abandoned all heroic thoughts of returning the key before Big Grandma woke up, and lay down to sob. A minute later she sat up again, and knew what had awakened her.

Smoke. She sniffed again. Definitely smoke. It smelled stronger lying down, but even when she sat up again it was still quite definite. Reaching under the bed she pulled out the candle stump she had stowed there after the escape from the storeroom, half expecting it to be still smouldering, but it was completely out. Peering across the room she could see Naomi's, lying on the bedside rug beside the dark heap that was her best dress. What had Rachel done with hers?

Rachel's candle had been forgotten. For a while it had stood gallantly upright by the pile of comics in the deserted room, and then a paper had slipped and knocked it sideways so that the wax dripped hotly onto the open pages Rachel had left behind her. A little later it fell completely, and the flaming wick spluttered in the pool of candle grease and the paper began to burn.

Slowly, because there was very little draught in the room, the comics charred and glowed, red in the center, smoking but hardly flaming. All the same, by the time they were reduced to white, harmless ashes, the wooden floor was alight. And then the fire was hot enough to burn cardboard, and then books.

Big Grandma's sleep grew deeper and deeper as the smoke curled through the cracks around the door which Ruth had very fortunately closed as they left. Except for an occasional quiet crack as the new timbers of the garage split and burned, the house was silent. Even the snoring had stopped.

By the time Ruth reached the door there was a blue haze of smoke hanging across the floor of Big Grandma's room and Big Grandma herself, despite being leaped upon, shaken, and screamed at by her eldest grand-daughter, only muttered in her sleep and refused to wake up.

"Is she dead?" Naomi arrived coughing at the door-

way, fending off Rachel and Phoebe who crowded behind her.

"Doped by smoke, I think," panted Ruth, and together she and Naomi, taking an arm and a leg each,
bumped Big Grandma out of bed and tugged her uncere-
moniously out onto the landing where Rachel and
Phoebe, in the mistaken apprehension that she was on
fire, poured toothmugs of water on her until she revived.

"Get her and the kids downstairs," ordered Naomi,
"while I phone for the fire brigade," and she closed
the bedroom door and flung herself down the stairs,
followed more slowly by Ruth, struggling to keep Big
Grandma upright without losing sight of Rachel and
Phoebe.

"What on earth is going on?" asked Big Grandma as
they lowered her onto a kitchen chair.

"The house is on fire," Phoebe told her gravely, but
rather tactlessly under the circumstances. Big Grandma
promptly complicated the situation by passing out.

"Is she dead?" It was Rachel who asked the question
this time.

"Fainted, I think. Help me prop her against the wall.
Look, she's coming around. Look after her while I find
Naomi." Ruth dashed out of the kitchen again leaving
Rachel trying to force Big Grandma to drink milk out
of the milk jug while Phoebe reassured her by saying,
"It's all right—only the upstairs is on fire. Ruth and
Naomi are sorting it out."

"ARE THEY COMING?" Ruth bumped into Naomi
in the hall.

"Be here any minute," Naomi replied. "It was awful. At first I couldn't remember the address or anything. Is Big Grandma okay? Where are the kids?"

"They're all in the kitchen. Rachel and Phoebe are looking after Big Grandma." Ruth spoke as she ran back up the stairs and Naomi followed after her, knowing what she was going to do.

Ruth paused for a second at Big Grandma's bedroom door. "I'm just going to try and get some of her books. You stay here. You've got a broken arm."

"So what?"

"So keep out." Ruth plunged through the blue smoke to the storeroom door and yanked it open. There was a bang like an explosion as the sudden rush of air fanned the slow fire into roof-high orange flames, and for a fraction of a second Ruth stared into a glare that was to stay in her nightmares for years, before, with Naomi's weight behind her, she crashed the door shut again and heard the floor of the storeroom fall through into the garage, and felt the old house shake as the garage roof tumbled down on top.

Down in the kitchen Rachel and Phoebe felt the crash and rushed to the foot of the stairs, calling for their sisters.

"Something awful's happened," said Rachel, as if something awful had not already been in progress for some time.

"I'm going up to see," Phoebe started to move away and Rachel grabbed her arm.

"Wait for me!" and "Do you think we'll die?" asked Rachel as they reached the landing and met Ruth and Naomi walking very slowly along the corridor.

208

The sight of their little sisters stirred Ruth and Naomi back into action.

"You're supposed to be looking after Big Grandma," yelled Naomi, turning Rachel around and running her back down the stairs.

"What about her books?" screamed Phoebe, trying to dodge under Ruth's arm. "You know it's all my fault!" Ruth grabbed her around the waist and carried her, loudly protesting, back into the kitchen.

The village arrived before the fire brigade, and even before they got there the fire was out, extinguished under the weight of the garage roof. Mr. Brocklebank, up before dawn to start the milking, had seen the glow of fire on the hillside, and arrived with Mark and Peter at the kitchen door at the same moment as the girls staggered wearily in from the hall.

"I don't think she's dead or anything," Ruth said as she saw them go to Big Grandma. "She wasn't a few minutes ago."

"She's been drinking milk and swearing," said Rachel.

"I'm fine." Big Grandma looked up and spoke for the first time as Mrs. Brocklebank and a frantic Graham dashed into the kitchen. "What about . . .?"

"The girls are all here," reassured Mrs. Brocklebank, with her arms around as many of them as she could hold.

"What about my books?" asked Big Grandma.

THE FIRE BRIGADE came and soaked the smoking ruins of the garage with several hundred gallons of water (thus destroying any books that might possibly have escaped the blaze). "Looks like you got off lightly," they said. "Nobody hurt and the fire hasn't touched the old house."

The policeman came, and, after hearing the story of how it had all started, remarked, "Somebody must have been watching over you last night. You've been very lucky." He got in his car to drive away, and then remembered something and came back to Ruth.

"Never, never open a door on a fire—it only fans the flames," he said. "Haven't they taught you that at school?" and when Ruth shook her head, "Well, I'm telling you now! Promise!"

"Yes, promise," said Ruth humbly. He was a nice man, but Ruth had already learned his lesson earlier that morning and had no intention of doing it twice.

The doctor said, "Might have been a tragedy."

"It is," said Big Grandma.

"Rubbish!" The doctor had seen real tragedies and knew the difference. "Nothing that a good night's sleep and the insurance won't cure! Do you want a sedative?"

"Certainly not!"

"You've got some smashing little lasses there," the doctor told her as he left.

All that morning, while people from the village cleaned the house, aired the rooms, took away smoky sheets and curtains to be washed and replaced them with fresh ones (some even taken from their own homes), brewed endless cups of tea, and brought huge supplies of food, Big Grandma had to listen to the same remarks.

"Lucky the wind was off the sea."

"Chap that put that garage up put it up to fall down."

"Good job he did, bit of luck she hadn't put the car in last night!"

"And you little lasses got your gran out of bed and down the stairs! You saved her life there you know!"

"And it was you phoned for the fire brigade!"

"And then the big ones went back to try and get the books she keeps on about!"

"And the little ones went to help them!"

"But it was us that started it!" protested Rachel through her tears. "It was my candle!"

"It was me that got the key." Phoebe could not look up for shame.

"It was all of us," said Naomi.

"And now we've burned her books!" and Ruth began sobbing again.

Mrs. Brocklebank had telephoned the girls' mother to say they would not be home that day after all, but would come on the following morning's train. Now she returned to hug the girls again and say, "Get a good night's sleep tonight, and go home smiling tomorrow! I've never heard so much fuss about a few books! Where's Graham's grandad got to?"

Graham's grandad was telling Big Grandma comforting stories of great fires he had witnessed. They all invariably ended in far greater calamity than Big Grandma had experienced and were full of idiots who kept their life savings in sacks of pound notes stuffed behind the stove, lit lanterns in stables and then got drunk and kicked them over, stacked their hay green, and smoked pipes in bed. "Didn't even find their bones," Mrs. Brocklebank heard him say as she came to fetch him home.

Graham lingered for a private farewell.

"I'll not be seeing you before you go," he said. "That

Sunday train leaves right early, and Mum says there's been enough fuss. I'll keep an eye on your gran."

"Thanks."

"She should have let you have them books in the first place."

"Don't say that, she might hear you."

"Not bothered if she does. And I'll see you next year."

"She'll never let us come back. She really does hate us now."

"Will you write to us?" asked Phoebe.

Graham, who would have cheerfully promised to rebuild the garage and bring Big Grandma to her senses, looked horrified at the proposal, but, as usual, found himself unable to refuse his friends' unreasonable request.

"I don't know. I might. If you write first."

"Yes."

"If I can think of anything to say. If I get time."

"All right."

"Bye then."

"Bye."

They watched him cycle away, saw him turn and wave, and heard him shout something over his shoulder.

"What's he say?"

"Said he wasn't marrying Rachel though," said Ruth.

"I don't suppose he wants to now," said Rachel sadly.

Nobody even smiled.

"WE'VE GOT to go in," said Ruth much later in the afternoon. "We've left her on her own too long as it is. We'll have to try and say sorry."

212

"I think I heard her crying," said Naomi. "I'm sure she was when Mrs. Brocklebank took her up."

"She was," Rachel nodded. "I saw her and she saw me seeing her. I couldn't help it."

The door that had opened into the dark little storeroom filled with a lifetime's collection of books now looked straight out onto the hillside, showing a picture of gold and purple heather and green waves of bracken. Big Grandma had opened the door, and now sat on her bed gazing silently through, while tears ran down her cheeks.

"Grandma," said Naomi, "we've come to say sorry."

"Very sorry."

Big Grandma did not even turn to look at them. "Go away."

"It was my candle," Rachel said bravely.

"Go right away."

"We can't tonight. Mrs. Brocklebank says there isn't a train. We'll go tomorrow, very early."

"We know where the tickets are. You don't need to get up or anything—we can easily go to the station ourselves."

"I took your key," Phoebe confessed. "I'm very, very sorry."

"We all are," said Ruth. "We'll go now. It was a lovely summer until yesterday."

It began to dawn on Big Grandma that they were saying good-bye, not just for the night or for the summer, but for always. An old memory of Robert flickered at the back of her mind.

"Thank you for having me," she heard Rachel say.

"It was lovely having you," said Big Grandma.

"Mrs. Brocklebank's got a brilliant supper all ready downstairs," said Rachel.

"YOU SEEM to have the sympathies of the entire village," said Big Grandma, some time later, when normal relationships had been resumed. "I suppose I ought to thank you for saving my life."

"That's okay," said Ruth.

"It was the least we could do," said Naomi.

"We'll get you some more books," Phoebe promised. "I'll use my Christmas-list money."

"You've still got my diary, and that Shakespeare," said Rachel.

"Things could be a lot worse," agreed Big Grandma.

"Graham said he'd keep an eye on you," Rachel told her, "but," she added honestly, "he won't be much use. He hasn't any books."

"Only three *Reader's Digests*," admitted Naomi.

"He promised *me* he'd keep an eye on *you*," said Big Grandma, "for fifty cents an hour I think it was."

"He's not charging us," said Ruth. "Is he still charging you? It must be a fortune by now!"

"He stopped charging after the first day," said Big Grandma.

Chapter 15

◀◀◀◀◀◀◀◀◀◀◀◀◀◀◀◀◀◀◀◀◀◀◀◀◀

"DEAR BIG GRANDMA," wrote Ruth.

Naomi and I have arranged to do the booktable for
the school bazaar. It was a bit hard because we are
in different classes. (Naomi should be selling cakes,
and she had to get herself thrown out of cookery),
but we have managed it so you will soon get a lot
of books. Some will be quite good because we
helped the English teacher sort out the library
stockroom (this was hard to arrange, too) and he
likes us. Did you know that in all the hurry I came
away without my bones. They are all packed and
ready so could you mail them?

Lots of love from Ruth

Dear Sir/Madam,

If you have finished with my diary could you send
it back now? These are from me and Phoebe. We

bought fifteen books at a sale, so now you have something to read.

Very much love and very sorry from Rachel

They are givin my Xmas list muny 50¢ a week for the rest of my life dad says so me and Rachel bort you these.

Love Phoebe Conroy

Dear Big Grandma,

I hope you got your insurance money, and that the lettuces and radishes I planted were all right. We didn't know Rachel and Phoebe hadn't put stamps on their books until too late. When they said they had made a long thin parcel, and squeezed it into the mailbox to fool the mailman we went to try and get it back, but it had gone. Luckily they were paperbacks, so they shouldn't cost you too much. Rachel and I have got you some very good books. But Mum says you will have to come and get them if you want them because there are fifty-seven.

You should see the house. Downstairs is fine, but all our rooms are pink (the curtains and sheets, and the walls) only with a dark gray carpet so as not to show the dirt. Mum asked what we thought. "It's a hellish pink," said Ruth for a joke. "You've come back worse," said Mum—but she was laughing.

So are you coming for Christmas?

Love Naomi

CPSIA information can be obtained
at www.ICGtesting.com
Printed in the USA
FSHW011305050119
54838FS